A Wilderness of Mirrors

Ed Cambro

Eloquent Books

New York, New York

Eloquent Books
An imprint of Writers Literary & Publishing Services, Inc.
845 Third Avenue, 6th Floor – 6016
New York, NY 10022
www.eloquentbooks.com

ISBN: 978-1-934925-52-2/SKU 1-934925-52-7

Printed in the United States of America

For my parents

And my eternal thanks to my friends Sal Pipitone and Jay Tilson, and everyone at Eloquent Books and the New York Literary Agency for taking a risk on some kid from Brooklyn.

"The optimist thinks this is the best of all possible worlds. The pessimist fears it is true."—J. Robert Oppenheimer

Table of Contents

1

Piedmont, Virginia

Dim light from the moon made the blood along the ground appear black; its round and gray presence reflected in the deep emptiness of the blood at certain points.

The blood was everywhere on the road: pools, streaks and hauled spatter. Deeper in the syrupy pools of black were the casings of bullets — the catalysts of the massacre.

The motorcade — comprised mostly of black humvees and military jeeps — had been stopped in the middle of its crossing, and were now garnished with bullet holes. The race up to the Skyline Drive in the Blue Ridge Mountains was winding, and for Bill Hamlin, Deputy Director of the FBI's Counter-terrorism Division, the cause of his nausea.

Hamlin and a group of CSI squints from Quantico traveled in their unmarked black Ford Excursions to the scene of the massacre, where Colonel Mitch Flynn and other members of the military were waiting.

Hamlin knew this was going to be a fight over jurisdiction. The military would want to investigate this matter themselves — it was their motorcade that was attacked, some kind of property of theirs stolen, and their officers killed. In all of his years in the FBI, it was a constant fight between agencies — federal, foreign, local and military, and it wasn't going to change. Hamlin took a quick chug of the small bottle of Pepto Bismol he had in the inside pocket of his coat, and exited the vehicle. They started to each other straight away; the pleasantry exchanged was that of a swift handshake. "When did you get in?" Hamlin asked.

"Five minutes ago."

The squints breezed past, getting to work immediately.

Flynn reacted. "This isn't your mandate."

"Complain to DNI Kirkland, or FBI Director Bowman. We've got the collar, so you might as well tell me what you know so far."

"A lot of what I know is classified." Hamlin scowled, but Flynn didn't give him chance to reply. "Twenty of our men — highly trained — were transporting a sensitive item to a location specified by the SecDef. The convoy was obviously ambushed. My soldiers were killed, the item stolen."

"Where are your men?" Hamlin was looking over Flynn's broad shoulders. "They don't seem to be… in the area."

"Follow me."

Squints down one side of the road were examining bloodied bodies — head shots, execution style.

"Jesus Christ on the cross."

"Isn't that where he usually is? We've accounted for nineteen out of twenty." Flynn said.

"So where do you think number twenty is?"

"We're searching the area. Are you implying something?"

"I don't want to, but I have to explore all the options."

"You mean the option of one of my men being involved in this."

"That's correct."

Flynn muttered something unintelligible under his breath.

"I'm only doing my job," Hamlin said.

One of the squints joined them. "We found number twenty."

The two men followed the squint to the other side of the road, on that side's downward slope. The soldier was laid out, double-tap to the head.

"Why do you think he was separated from the group?"

"There are signs of a struggle here," one squint said. "The ground is disturbed, like at least one person slid down, and the soldier's lip is bleeding, which is unrelated to the gunshot."

Flynn said to Hamlin, "Guess that thread didn't stretch too far,"

"Theft still seems to be the motive here. You ready to level with me?"

Above, a squint with a Geiger counter waded through the debris and wreckage. When he reached the center humvee the counter snapped to life and screamed.

The counter was heard just further down the valley where Hamlin now turned to the Colonel. He said, "Never mind."

2

Washington, D.C.

Secretary of Defense Alan Kersh received a phone call from FBI Deputy Director Bill Hamlin, who alerted him of the possibility of an attack. He was walking the halls of the White House on the way to the Oval Office for a meeting with the President and his Chief of Staff.

"What the hell is going on?" President Ellison said sleepily. Beside him was Chief of Staff Ronald Kurtzweil.

"A military convoy was ambushed in Virginia," Kersh reported. "Twenty men were reported as killed, and the item the convoy was moving was stolen."

"The nuclear device?" Ellison asked.

"Yes, sir."

"By God," Kurtzweil murmured.

"Do we have any leads?"

"The Bureau is running point — they're working ballistics on the bullets found in the soldiers. They're hoping it will generate more leads."

"So there's nothing else. No suspects?"

"Nothing as of yet."

"How could they have gotten the information about the convoy let alone where it was going and what it was carrying?" Ellison asked.

"Frankly, sir, I don't know. Perhaps once we find out who masterminded this."

Ellison stood from his seat, turned to the window behind him — predawn outside. "We need to smother this — keep it from the public. Did we get anything off satellite?"

"Nothing sir, we had no satellite coverage in the area at the time."

"Christ — I said I wanted the convoy covered."

The room was silent for a long moment. Ellison deliberated. "Have NEST deployed," Ellison ordered. "Tell them this one's for real."

NEST stood for Nuclear Emergency Support Team, in charge of responding to any radiological crisis anywhere in the world. They were the best at what they did.

"I also want all agencies put on high alert; the threat level raised — to Elevated."

"Sir, we should also consider bringing in Interpol — see if they've heard anything on their end," Kurtzweil added.

Ellison nodded, his features obviously strained. The truth of the matter was simple: this could make 9/11 look like a schoolyard brawl.

3

Manhattan, New York

From here, Besson thought, you would actually think the city was urbane.

He was looking down onto the city — which seemed somehow naked without the Towers, even after all these years — from the field branch of Halifax, the nation's fourth-largest defense contractor.

Below him, the bridges glowed; the taller buildings were black citadels with dozens of tiny eyes at their side, all burning into the night, an amazing electric city that made the black sky bright, almost alive. However, down further from the lights and spiraling towers was a majority whose lives were in question.

The truth to Besson had been illuminated for him some time ago: in order for things to change, people — good or bad — must die.

Of course, it didn't have to come to this, Besson thought. There were thousands of possibilities to choose from in the wake of September 11th. We'd happened to choose poorly. Had we chosen a slightly more peaceful resolution — rather than becoming an imperial force and turning America into one of the most hated nations on earth — the plan Besson had created would never have been conceived, let alone put into play.

"I know that look," said a voice from behind. "It's the look of a man who could use a drink."

Besson turned and faced Martin Frederick Strughold, the CEO of Halifax, who was chuckling at his joke, as he did often.

"I was waiting for you. Drinking alone is too brooding. Like a late-in-life Bruce Wayne would do."

Strughold went for the small bar in the corner of the office —it was his office they were in — and made them drinks. "JD as always?"

"You know it."

Strughold was, for an armchair warrior, surprisingly large. At six-four and wide shouldered, and showing the weight of his age, he was particularly imposing — a strong advantage in his business. "I don't know how you drink it, Will. I've always been a vodka man myself."

"Well, you know what they say, vodka's for girls."

Both men chuckled. Strughold handed him his glasses and raised his own. "To a job well done."

Their glasses clinked, and they took heavy gulps of their drinks.

Strughold said, "I was just on the phone with Moira. She said the bomb wasn't damaged in the process of the extraction."

"Good. I'm surprised that we haven't heard anything about this on the news yet."

"Considering the time of year it is I don't think Ellison wants that kind of attention just yet." He paused. "Want to tell me your version of what happened?"

"Been a week already. Why ask now?"

"There are a lot of stories out there about it. I want yours."

Besson sighed. "Went down exactly as I planned — at first. We stopped them — a van in front, one in back. We all poured out, had them drop their weapons and line up, single file. One gets the slip and makes a break for it down one side of the road. I dove after him, we fought and he got my mask off — saw my face. There was no other alternative. Double-tap in the head. As I got up to the main road Anderson had decided my orders were null and void. Ordered his hillbilly boys to open fire. Executed all of them."

Strughold eyed Besson who was circling the bottom of the glass. "You don't like the way it went down,"

"It was needless and stupid on my part. I knew I couldn't trust Anderson by himself, but I left him up there anyway. But yeah, I regret having to kill that soldier and I regret letting the others get killed too."

"The soldier gave you no choice. He saw your face and if you let him live he might've made you. It was a... reasonable course of action."

"Doesn't make it right."

"Did you let Anderson and his boys take the guns?"

"That was the deal."

"Good, we're still going to need to use him and his militia."

"I know," Besson sighed. "Son of a bitch."

"You'll get the last laugh on him in the end, believe me. I need you on a plane —speaking of— within the next few days, back down to Nevada. We're entering the next phase and we still need Anderson on board." Strughold finished his vodka, offered a refill. Besson handed him his glass. "I'll be leaving the country for a short time, and then I'm going back to D.C. Until I get back Peter will be your provisional handler."

Besson smiled wryly, then said, "Thanks for the bureau jargon."

Strughold laughed. "Thought you'd appreciate it." He paused for a long moment. "I don't want to sound doubtful, but there's something I just want to bring up."

"What's that?" Besson asked.

"The soldier was just one person, his brigade was another twenty or so. When this bomb goes off there will be millions killed. Are you going to be okay with that?"

"Never. But it needs to be done."

"I know this must be tough on you, the gravity of what we're doing here," he said as he placed a hand on Besson's shoulder, "but you have to see that you're a hero, right? You're doing the right thing; and sometimes doing the right thing isn't the prettiest thing to do."

Besson nodded. "It's not supposed to be."

A pause, then Strughold went off the topic. "I honestly can't still believe your password at the CTD was still active."

"The information was old and the Division is always backlogged. Besides, the Bureau has more priorities than canceling my password."

Strughold glanced at his watch. "It's almost time."

The two men sauntered back to the window, peered out at the city.

"I've only seen it on TV or in pictures, never up close," Strughold said.

From below, two white beams of light streaked into the night sky. The effect of the svelte and simple appearance of the twin peaks was omnipresent; they loomed over the city with a strong solemnity that was felt wholly by anyone who looked upon them.

At its foundation, a mass of onlookers and mourners had been gathering since the early morning, as they do every year on this day. They were the ones who fought the ravages of a collective mentality that was a short-term memory, those who fought change. They were the ones that chose and fought hard never to forget.

The city felt heavier, then — battle worn. Deep inside the soul of the sleek conurbation was the memory of slamming steel and ash, like the operatic chorus and curtain call on the closing days of a falling empire.

Besson said, "Me neither."

4

The FBI's Manhattan field office was maintained by its key personnel: Assistant Director David Graham, Andrea Jansen — the lead field agent and defacto SAC, and her partner Jim Dormer. Elizabeth Tess was the head technical analyst and Don Walker served as the communications expert.

Jansen stepped off the elevator and walked into the main office, which was down a long gray hallway where the restrooms, conference room, storage closets and interrogation rooms were found. Beyond that hallway, there were two pane-glass sliding electronic doors, which opened as Jansen entered the cluttered office. There were no cubicles in the office, all open desks, with people constantly fluttering about. At the back of the office, there were two offices; David Graham's and a smaller office for Jansen.

The dark haired, heavy-set Jim Dormer dressed in a blue button down shirt and a navy blue blazer met Jansen as she passed through the sliding doors.

"What's the situation?" Jansen asked, knowing that Dormer would be there waiting for her. "Is it about the stolen nuke?"

"No — DC is taking us off it," Dormer reported in his usual raspy tone. "They're taking the lead on it. There's something else. NSA is predicting that an attack is imminent, separate from the nuke. Nobody even knows who has that damned thing, anyway."

"When?"

"Soon."

"*Soon?*"

"They said that's all they knew and that there's definitely gonna be an attempt within the next few weeks, but nobody seems to know when yet."

"How did NSA get the Intel?"

"Anonymous tip told us to look into the name Alexis Ravens. We did. A large amount of C-4 bought in Mexico. The sellers' name was Alexis

Ravens. As it goes, Ravens was under investigation by Mexican authorities. The JTTF pinched him trying to cross the border.

"When questioned he was told that he could spend the rest of his life in prison for treason — he's an American citizen no less — and he flipped fifteen minutes after that. In exchange for immunity, he chewed everyone's ears out about all the people he had sold to; including the joker that bought the C-4. Turns out, the buyer was also very chatty, told Ravens that he was going to use the C-4 to hit New York."

"Does Ravens know what group this guy might belong to? Or his name or at least a description for that matter?" Jansen asked.

"No name, but the guy mentioned he lives in Vegas."

"Did Ravens give them a description?"

"Yeah, they had Ravens talk to a sketch artist. A copy of it is on your desk, along with all the information they have so far."

"Something doesn't seem right about this. It's too *easy*."

"Maybe we're getting lucky."

"I'll believe it when I see it. Where's the C-4 now?"

"Ravens said it'd be in America by now."

"Thank you, Homeland Security. Where's Graham?"

"I don't know."

"Well, find him, and tell him what you just told me. Meanwhile, I'm gonna call Washington."

"Why?"

"The Secretary of Defense is supposed to be coming into town soon to make a speech at the U.N. He might want to put it off for a few weeks until we put out this fire. Between this and the missing nuke we could be looking at major shitstorm."

"Well at least the nuke is the military's fault and not the Bureau's."

"Yeah, we'll just take the hit for the plastic. And Jim?"

"Yeah?"

"Do you know how much C-4 was sold?"

"Two truckloads."

"Christ on the cross. Alright, contact local PD; we're going to need to coordinate with them. Don't tell them too much, just to keep their eyes open."

"Got it."

"I'm going to conference with DC. And, Jim?"

"Yeah?"

"*Find Graham.*"

5

Pahrump, Nevada

They didn't speak much over flight or the drive over, besides the usual pleasantries, which, even then, were kept to a minimum.

Out in the desert-like land owned by Josh Anderson were a series of bunkers, which Besson was quickly driving toward. From the bunkers circles of reflected light from the sun glared white-hot at Besson and his passenger, Peter Lavalle.

"I don't like that." Lavalle was, in his youth, a former French Legionnaire who had went into business for himself as a mercenary for hire after leaving the service. Business had been good for him, as his career in the underground spanned two decades and had taken him around the world. Over the last year, however, he found himself settled in America, in the deep pockets of Martin Frederick Strughold.

"Their using the guns we gave them," Besson said.

"They know we are coming, don't they?"

"Yes, but that doesn't fill me with much confidence. Maybe I should wave my underwear out the window, show we're friendly."

"Thank God for white underwear, eh?" Lavalle mused.

"If they don't calm down, they won't be that way much longer." Besson waved a hand out the window and slowed to a stop.

Josh Anderson stepped out from one of the bunkers, a shit-kicking grin on his face as a hand through his thick blonde hair. Anderson was the leader of a militia whose intentions were to overthrow the government and start fresh — reformatting the country in the way that the Forefathers intended; hence the militia's name: The Sons of Liberty. Anderson was nothing if not an excellent historian.

Anderson and those likeminded felt that the current America had veered too far from what the country was intended to be. Anderson and his cohorts considered themselves to be patriots, saving America from the evil of itself.

The FBI thought differently. Anderson had made their Watch List in 1995 but failed to capture him. Following 9/11 the priority to bring him in dwindled, as focus shifted toward other persons of interest. Anderson woke up every morning knowing this fact and took full advantage.

"Glad to see you're making use of the guns we gave you," Lavalle said. "The glare from the scopes is blinding us, why don't you point them someplace else."

"Like where?"

"I could suggest a few places," Besson replied.

Anderson flashed a toothy grin. He waved his well-toned and muscular arm behind him and the glare disappeared. "So what do you boys want?"

"Job offering," Lavalle said.

"What kind of job, Pete?"

"*Peter*. High stakes, high reward."

"Bigger than stealing government tech and killing Gestapo?"

"Much."

"What're you offering?"

"Eight million," Besson said. "And we're supplying the explosives."

"You don't trust my people for that?"

"The last time I did twenty innocent ones died needlessly."

"Just taking the Gestapo down a peg."

"Always fighting the good fight," Besson responded wryly.

"Somebody has to."

"Do you want the job or not?"

"Details, boys. Details."

Five miles west of the compound was Skeet — a rundown hellhole of a bar whose floor breathed the stale aroma of spilt beer, sweat and vomit. The air permeated the smell of cigarettes, as well as a thin fog.

The bartender was a former Hells Angel, as his tattoos implied (though he'd break the teeth of anyone who asked).

Lavalle gleefully freed a Dunhill from its wide pack and lit up. He still hadn't gotten used to the severe restrictions Americans had placed on public smoking. Anderson called for some drinks, and as the bartender turned his bald head into the direction of the tap, Lavalle noticed a warning written on an old chalkboard: NO GIVING HEAD IN THE HEAD.

"Ahh, the wiles and charms of the proletariat."

The bartender brought the beers around; Anderson was the only one who drank. "So tell me what the job is," he said.

"We want you to carry out an attack we've designed."

"Just don't tell me this is a rehash of OKC, because that was Timmy's thing, not ours."

"We want you to hit the Manhattan Bridge."

"Why?"

"Bigger picture," Besson said.

"Paint it for me."

"If it's all the same to you, I think I'll pass."

"No, we should tell him," Lavalle interjected. "You want to strike the government, don't you?"

Anderson nodded.

"By hitting New York, it'll open the old 9/11 wounds and rile the people up, get them mad at their leaders for letting it happen again. With the focus shifting back to New York, we'll strike the real target in the real city."

Anderson's interest was piqued. He was almost out of his chair.

"The Pentagon," Lavalle revealed.

Anderson smiled wide.

"So are you interested?" Besson asked after a long moment.

"Deal."

A cab waited for Besson outside the bar. He climbed inside the backseat when Anderson knelt beside the window.

"You really don't trust me." Anderson stated.

"You're a reckless animal and I don't see what your motives are."

"We're patriots, like you."

"I'm nothing like you."

"I told you: if we didn't kill them, they would have gotten back to the base and fucked us all."

"That's bullshit. It was a power play, bravado in front of your boys. You're a murderer."

A wink and a jackal's grin, "Don't forget — one of their number was yours." Anderson made a gun with his fingers and made a clicking sound. He tapped the roof of the cab and it sped away, Besson looking gaunt.

6

Sleep didn't come quickly for Will Besson on his flight back to New York. As he drifted he knew he would be met by his most recent memory of shame. When he finally fell asleep, as he had presupposed he would, he returned to Virginia.

...the soldiers slowly filed out, fingers interlocked behind their heads, and walked towards the first van. The section of soldiers to the maximum left walked along the edge of the road where it slid down into the valley. One soldier from that section stepped from his ranks, ducked, and allowed himself to slide down the slope into the valley in a vain attempt to escape.

The first soldier's dissension started an uprising, which was quickly halted with the threat of violence and several warning shots bursting from random Sons members.

Besson pursued, tumbling down the slope, and losing his MP-5 in the process. He veered forward as he slid down the hillside and pushed upward with his knees, diving at the escaping soldier who tumbled back down with him to the bottom of the valley. Still on the ground, Besson grabbed at the soldier who was attempting to stand. Besson was met with a sharp elbow to the temple. The soldier faced Besson, and attempted to ram his head in the ground, but lost his grip as Besson pushed him away, accomplishing only the removal of Besson's ski mask. The soldier had been taken off balance, and Besson kicked him away and in one motion, stood up, drew and cocked his dual-tone SIG-Sauer P228, and pointed it at the now humbled and motionless soldier.

For a long moment the two men stared blankly. The soldier had nowhere to run and no way of defending himself anymore. They both panted in fatigue and shared the wish for the day to end already. The unmasked Besson and the soldier both knew the implications for the action the soldier had taken. Besson's face was in full view — the soldier had a very good look at him and would be able to recount an excellent likeness to a sketch artist. Besson hesitated. He knew the soldier was only trying to do his job and complete his work, and he had no idea of the details of the plan. He was totally innocent to everything around him, and he was only guilty of seeing another man's face. The soldier told Besson that he had a wife and children. Unfortunately, small though it may seem, the soldier's crime was punishable by death, and for Besson's sense of self-preservation he had no choice but to carry out the soldier's sentence. Besson fired twice as the soldier was in the middle of screaming Wait!

A dreadful guilt burned down Besson's chest. The only other person he had killed had, in his opinion, deserved it, but the man lying before him was innocent of any wrongdoing. Due to the Kevlar vest the soldier wore, Besson had to fire two headshots, and as a result his family wouldn't even be able to give him an open casket funeral.

His family.

Into the short distance, back on the main road Besson heard the compressed sounds of gunfire, more specifically MP-5 gunfire that rattled down the valley to Besson's position.

He quickly scaled back up the hillside to see the other soldiers all dead —all lined up facing the mountainside and shot, execution style.

The inexorable truth: There would be more than one closed casket funeral in the near future.

7

Manhattan, New York

She was caught off guard seeing him. He didn't look all that different, not that two years would change much of a person's appearance.

He was tall, his broad shoulders wrapped in the same leather jacket he'd had for years. His eyes, under a healthy wave of auburn hair, scanned the room, cataloging specific faces and noteworthy details. His walk was still narrow and his arms were still curved as he walked so he could always make a quick grab for his service weapon, though nowadays he didn't carry it around with him. It had been two years since his departure from the FBI — two years since he left her, six years down the drain — and his stride and carriage still reflected the agent he had once been.

She thanked God for having decided to take the booth in the odd corner of the bar, from where she could look out without others being able to look in at her. It gave her the advantage of seeing him before he saw her, letting her decide what was to be her next move.

She could wait it out, but not for too long since she was expected at the office soon. She could wait until his head was down, either in a menu or in his food, and hope for a speedy and unnoticed exit. He was halfway through his bacon cheeseburger when she decided she could just go up to him.

Besson's new home was a Whitestone building with wrought-iron gates, across the street from Hunter College. Strughold forwarded Besson a great deal of money and paid his rent in full for several months.

Just inside the door there was a narrow hallway to the left where, on the right there was a full bathroom. All the way down the hall, in the center, there was the bedroom. To the right there was a large living room. The living room had a long couch going along the wall with one window at each end. In the middle was a door leading out to the balcony. Just beyond the living room was a small counter to the other end of the apartment where there was a kitchen, dining room and a den.

On the wall just to the left of the kitchen, Besson had placed his bookshelf, and to the right was his computer. On the wall above the television he'd hung the accommodation he received for capturing Ludlow Kealty, which he realized happened almost ten years ago. He sighed, feeling his age.

His bedroom had a closet, which held the rest of the FBI accoutrements that Besson had accumulated over the years. There was also a chest of drawers, and under his bed a shoebox where he kept his loaded SIG, with two extra clips beside it.

He toured the city quite often at this time, saying final goodbyes to places that would never be seen again — places that would be relegated to his memory, no longer under the aegis by what used to be his sense of right and wrong. Central Park, the Metropolitan museum, Times Square, Union Square, all the places he had long since damned.

John Jay College had changed quite a bit since his days as a student. It had taken on more property, expanded. As he walked down 55th street he smiled when spotted McGee's Pub, a traditional Irish pub that had served as Besson's second home and party base as a student.

Scanning the interior as he walked in he noticed the burgundy contours of the bar — its seats, the walls, the general motif — hadn't changed, though the lighting was brighter, more welcoming. The seat at the bar that had at one time been specifically designated as his was occupied, and decided to take a seat in a booth.

An unfamiliar waitress eventually came to ask for his order. On reflex, he almost said "the usual," but instead he sighed to himself with the trace of a smirk and said, "Bacon cheeseburger deluxe — cooked medium — with a coke and a slice of cherry pie."

From the first bite he was taken back to his youth, and was hoping one of his favorites would come on the radio to make the memory perfect.

From over the smell of the burger, the scent of jasmine filled his nostrils and a voice broke his daydream. "Will." He sat, agape.

She was just as attractive as he had remembered — a slender, beautiful woman, high cheek bones, long, shapely legs, flowing blonde hair, styled so that it often covered one eye. And her eyes. Aqua blue, an ocean of opportunity. They were vast and kind. He was still as fascinated with her as he was when they met. The smell of her hair, her body, had the faint smell of jasmine which danced in Besson's nostrils and he felt again entranced by her. "Andrea," Besson whispered.

"Small world, isn't it?" Jansen said with a genuine smile. "It's good to see you." She was in a pants suit — work attire that she was often confined to.

Besson stood to greet her. The two shook hands, laughed awkwardly, then hugged. She could tell Besson felt he owed her more than a business-like handshake.

Jansen had to hold her handbag from falling off her shoulder when they embraced. The black handbag she wore was appropriately large, so she could keep her service weapon, a Glock .45 automatic handgun, in it without it being noticed when she was on the street. It was currently with her.

"Yeah, you too. How are you?" Besson asked, more aware and focused. "You're working in New York now?"

"Yeah, I'm the SAC of the Manhattan field office."

Besson's interest was piqued. "Anything fun happening there?"

"A lot of things, never much fun. Usually just some tip from a guy who was mad that his Arabic speaking cabbie made him late."

"A little far from the office though, aren't you? Or are you investigating another cabbie?"

Jansen laughed. "No, I was doing a guest speaker spot for Mark Rosen's Terrorism and the Law class at John Jay."

"The former DA?"

"The one and only."

"I just passed by there." He laughed. "If I'd known I would've gone in and bothered him."

"Is it different from what you remember? John Jay, I mean. Not the… bothering… people…" She trailed off, wondered if she had recently taken drugs.

"The entire city is different, but still like it used to be," Besson said.

"Isn't that a contradiction?"

Besson laughed. "That's what happens here. New York is an entirely different world, isn't it?"

"That's what I'm looking for. What brings *you* to New York?"

"I'm living here again, just got back a few months ago," Besson replied carefully.

Jansen's cell phone rang just then and she answered, with obvious frustration. She spoke briefly and tensely with the person on the other line, hung up, and looked at Besson. "There goes my lunch break, but listen; would you like to get a bite sometime? Tonight, or during the week or something?"

Jansen heard herself speaking as if she were outside her body; she didn't know why she said it and she couldn't stop herself.

Besson hesitated. "Sure, I'm free."

"Great." She handed him her card. "My cell phone number's on back. Call me after eight-thirty."

"Sure, sounds great." Then genuinely, "It was good to see you."

"Yeah, you too."

Once at home, Besson realized the potential of having a friend inside the Bureau who could feed him torrents of information without even realizing what she's actually doing. Tactically, it was a good decision; especially considering that the FBI had finally deactivated his code. The thought suddenly stopped him, and left him feeling guilty for coming up with the idea in the first place. He decided that he would ask her only one or two questions — simple questions — that would just ease his mind and leave her none the wiser. He still didn't like having to deceive her, but as most of his unpleasant duties of late, it was necessary.

Head staff members Andrea Jansen, Jim Dormer, Elizabeth Tess and Don Walker filed into the conference room where David Graham was already sitting at the head of the table. He seemed alert, the sweat that usually decorated his forehead had dissipated, and his eyes were again like fire. The conference room was surrounded in pane-glass framing, with flat-screen monitors flashing with items of importance hanging from the ceiling and around the walls. The table in the center of the room had stationary laptops at each seat, so anyone could bring up any file or program from their own computers and use it in the room once their code was punched in. Due to the heavy reliance of visual images on screens, the room was dimly lit to avoid glare, as it usually was.

The side of David Graham's face and his salt and pepper hair appeared blue from the tinting of the light coming off his laptop.

"As you already know by now," he began, "the threat level is being raised and the likelihood of an attack seems to be greater than it has been in a while. We are expecting an attack or at least an attack within the next few weeks. All major cities are under high alert, but New York seems to be the target, as stated by Alexis Ravens. Washington has put us in charge of the investigation and we have been ordered to tighten our grip." Graham nodded to Jansen. "Go ahead."

Jansen projected a list onto the laptops on the table. "In case of an attack, this is a list of several likely locations whose probability of being hit is higher than any other locations in Manhattan. I have informed all agencies, both local and federal, that security is to be tightened at these locations. I've also contacted the FAA and they're going to watch air traffic for any small or low-flying aircraft and airports are being ordered do more 'random searches'."

"Shouldn't they be doing that anyway?" Walker asked.

"Yes, but they tend to get lazy."

"Contact the Air Force and put them on alert," Graham said to Walker. Then to the room, "Another attack from the sky is unlikely but not impossible. In the minds of terrorists if it worked once, it will work again. In case they are attacking from the air I want the Air Force standing by to shoot the obstacle or obstacles down. Any progress on identifying the man who bought the C-4?"

"The Las Vegas office sent us a copy of the sketch and they're cross checking their databases for a match," Dormer said.

"You told me that earlier, Jim. It's old news. I want you to cross check *our* databases for a match on this guy. Confer with the Vegas mainframe if you have to. Don, keep in close touch with them. If they get this guy I want to find out thirty seconds beforehand. I also want someone from our side over there working with Vegas who could report back to us."

"I'll call Hamlin and ask for more personnel," Jansen said.

"Try to get a guy who already has ties with Vegas and has good relations with our friends," Graham ordered. "I also want all the people on the NCTC list under heavy surveillance, with teams ready to roll on them in a moments notice. Liz, how are our systems functioning? Are there any hackers trying to breach our systems?"

"No more than usual."

"I want to find some of these hackers, and rattle the cages. How is the Internet chatter?"

"It's raised, but not high enough to assume anything."

"Find out why it's raised. Where are we as far as damage control and emergency response time?"

"There's not much to say… I don't know where the bombing is going to take place. I've been running a broader simulation, but with no idea where to approximate ground zero, I can't…"

"Damnit, Liz, I don't want excuses! Did Andrea give you this list earlier?"

"Yes."

"Then you don't have a reason to not have the work done."

"David, it's still a hard task — the simulations will still take longer than the half hour you've given me."

"This has to be done with quickly. We cannot allow another attack on American soil, let alone another one in *this city*. If this attack goes through, terrorists will declare it open season on this country, and then it will be a world of shit." Then, sarcastically, "So I'm sorry if the pressure is getting to you, but I'll remind you that potentially millions of lives are at risk here." There was an extended silence which Graham also broke. "How about overseas? How many cells in Europe would target us?"

"Twelve as of last year," Jansen replied. "However, British and French agencies have begun to crack down, especially since the subway bombing. I've made some calls and I'm waiting on an update."

"I'll call the Vegas field office in Washington and see if they could tell us anything," Walker said.

Graham's mind had been wandering. He realized the Valium he'd taken hadn't begun to take effect, and it should have by then. He began to consider taking two before work everyday or having his doctor increase the dosage. Jansen noted the perspiration on Graham's head had returned as well as his flushed cheeks. She thought it was a fever.

"With all that C-4," Graham asked slowly, "what could it do to a large building or a bridge?"

"It'll take a building down like Oklahoma City, and it would blow a substantial chunk of a bridge off," Dormer reported. "That's if they're using the C-4 for just one attack. If they decide to attack multiple places, it'll be a whole new ball game."

"I'm working on that right now," Tess said. "Likely targets in case of multiple attacks — what places would be targeted and how much C-4 would need to be used."

"Good, I want that on everyone's desk as soon as it's done." Graham looked at the screen of his laptop. "Delivery system?"

"Other than by air, the best way would be by truck or planted bomb," Jansen said. "We could check the bags of everyone that comes into buildings we flag as likely targets for attack, as well as search any suspicious vehicles in the area, with bomb sniffing dogs on hand."

Graham nodded, and turned to Tess, "I'm going to need figures on how much manpower this will take, so confer with Andrea on this. When you get an approximate figure, Andrea, I want you to call Bill Hamlin at Quantico."

Graham was silent for several seconds. When he spoke again his voice was low and careful. "We are expecting a head-on attack, much like the Oklahoma City bombing, and millions of lives are on the line, not to mention the security of the rest of the nation. Now is the time to prove ourselves out here. We have to find the C-4 and the people carrying it before these terrorists can complete their mission. All other concerns are secondary."

Jansen and Dormer sat at Tess's desk, and the three of them revised the target list to meet Graham's specifications.

"Do you think they might use it in a subway station like in Madrid or London?" Dormer asked.

"Probably not," Tess said. "Security is pretty high, and it's only going to get harder for them to smuggle something into the subway if Hamlin approves the new security outline."

"*If*," Dormer muttered.

"Graham already called the MTA and they're beefing up security for the time being with their own people, and the NYPD has added some support teams at the LIRR, Penn Station and Grand Central, and the PATH train," Jansen said.

"Then what do you need me for?" Dormer asked wryly.

In the same wry tone, Jansen replied, "Eye candy for the press."

"The list is pretty big," Tess reported. "It'll be about an hour before the computer is done compiling everything."

"Just get the 'worst case scenario' statistics in that case," Jansen ordered. "Quantico wants it in a half hour. Then work on the rest."

"The NCTC identified the buyer and is sending us the information," Walker announced. He activated the large teleprompter at the back of the office as everyone brought their attention to it. "His name is Josh Anderson."

"I want the names of everyone Anderson has been connected to over the last four years, and I want the names of the cells he's suspected of having dealings with," Jansen ordered.

Graham, who had stepped out his office once the teleprompter had been activated, looked at his watch, and took the cell phone from his ear. He motioned Jansen to join him.

"Is something wrong, David?"

"No, everything's fine. Listen, something's come up. Personal. You're in charge. I'll have my cell phone with me if anything."

"David, now is not the time to —"

Quietly, but with a forceful anger, "*Just do the fucking job.*"

"Yes… *sir.*"

"What the hell was that about?" Dormer muttered to Tess, after watching Graham storm out.

Jansen joined them back at Tess' station.

"He does this every week," Tess replied. "At least one day a week he leaves, twice, and is gone for about an hour or two."

"And how do you know this?" Jansen asked.

"Because he borrows a field vehicle — I go over the records every week. He's had this routine a while," Tess replied.

"We can gossip later," Jansen muttered. Then to the rest of the office, "I want everything done as quickly as possible. Work together, divide workloads, I don't care how, just do it. I want status reports every half hour, with copies of our progress reports sent to AD Graham's computer, mine and Quantico. Remember — this is the big time everyone, let's not lose any more buildings than we already have."

As her thoughts shifted back to her most recent encounter with David Graham, Jansen realized how good she had become at keeping her opinions to herself.

8

Amidst the booming sound system blasting out classic rock songs, Andrea Jansen walked up the stairs to the second level of the Hard Rock Café on Columbus Circle at ten p.m. that night. She was still wearing her customary work clothes, and was shown to her table where Will Besson was already waiting and had already ordered a drink, which she knew immediately was a jack and coke — his favorite.

Besson was wearing blue jeans and a beige button-down shirt with the sleeves slid up. His leather jacket hung over the back of his chair. Besson noticed her, stood up and greeted her with a handshake that turned to a kiss on the cheek and a smile.

"Sorry I'm late," Jansen said.

"Its okay, I'm a bit of a night owl myself."

A waitress handed them menus while Jansen ordered a scotch.

"Were you waiting long?"

"Not at all," Besson said, lifting his glass. "See? I'm still on my first drink."

They both chuckled lightly at Besson's joke, slightly awkward, with a slight hint of the sexual tension that remained since the first time they met.

"How is it working here?"

"Really hectic. I just settled into the office last year and between the problems in equipment, the lack of personnel, and having to beef up security on the subways and for the World Series coming up, things have been non-stop." Jansen sighed. "But enough about work."

"Yeah. Do you like living in New York?"

"It's... *new*. I've never been to New York, let alone Manhattan, so it's all a bit of a shock."

"Yeah, but do you like it?"

"I think I do. It's just the hustle and bustle that got to me at first, you know?"

"I almost forgot about it. I was in my twenties when I left for the FBI and when I came back it took some getting used to again." Besson chuckled. "I used to hate the commute going into the city."

"I usually drive in."

"I wish I had a car during college."

"Me too." She skipped a beat, then said, "I'm sure I asked this before, but how long've you been back in New York?"

"Not long, a few weeks."

"Where are you living now?"

"Across the street from Hunter College, one of the Whitestone buildings."

"That's a great area."

"It was a dream of mine as a kid to live in a place like that." Besson smiled, reliving that memory. Jansen smiled lightly at the sentimentality.

When the waitress returned, Besson ordered a steak and Jansen ordered a turkey club. Both ordered refills for their drinks.

"What've you been up to since you left DC?" Jansen asked.

Besson, unprepared for the question, but assuming he would've had to answer the question eventually, simply said, "Lotta nothing."

"Fun never stops with you, does it."

Besson chuckled. "Never,"

The waitress returned with their drinks, and there was a silence in which the two of them focused on their drinks intently.

"Not to get off track here," Jansen said, "and you don't have to answer me if you don't want to, but what happened in that Career Board that made you quit the Bureau?"

Besson took several long gulps, then said, "They didn't approve of the things I did. You know, booze, broads, and bucars."

Jansen laughed.

"Don't get me wrong — I got results, you know that. But they didn't like the way I got those results." Besson took another sip of his drink, and then said dryly, "And I think they were going to recommend me for the Rampart Division in L.A." Besson smirked.

"Can I ask you something, Will?"

"Shoot."

"Why did you leave?"

He knew this was coming. She had every right to know. Not long after leaving the Bureau, he left Andrea — and their six-year relationship. After a reflective pause, Besson said, truthfully and slowly, "I was at a crossroad and needed to clear my head." Another pause. "I guess you could say the circumstances were the circumstances. I couldn't get past what happened, with the Board and all, and I felt I had no where to turn. I mean, the Bureau was all I ever knew, and all I ever wanted. After all the work I did for them, all my sacrifices for the Bureau, they hung me out to dry. It was... disheartening."

"You had me. You had me and you had Carl."

"I know, and I screwed up. I think I just went kind of, I dunno... I think I had a midlife crisis."

"Do you still talk to Carl?"

"I've tried. He hasn't talked to me since I quit. He was pretty mad." He paused. "I thought about calling you a few times."

"When?"

"Every day."

Their hands were on the table, touching, and they both noticed it at the same time, and pulled back from each other.

There was an awkward pause and Jansen looked back up at Besson to say something but the waitress had returned with their orders. They ate in silence for several minutes. The air needed to clear.

"What do you do now?" Jansen asked.

"I work for the branch office of Halifax here in Manhattan."

"Really? As what?"

"Consultant."

"It's far from being at the Bureau."

"That's what I'm looking for."

"You really want to slow your life down, don't you?"

"I knew people in the Bureau who lived the same fast-paced life I did, and I know for a fact that they would sell their souls to go back in time and slow the pace down."

"What happened to them?"

"Nothing good, I'll tell you. Alcohol rehab, divorces… more divorces."

Besson paused, not really wanting to, but realizing it was important, and asked Jansen about the convoy that was attacked, which had made news the world over by then. The "stolen tech," however, remained a secret to the public.

"The investigation is being headed up by the DC office, since it's their jurisdiction."

"Do you think it could be a bomb someone's using to strike at us?"

"We considered it, and we're watching smuggling rings closer now. All we could do is wait and see, and hope we get lucky. I just don't know what 'lucky' is in this situation; finding it here or not."

Both laughed.

"That's what we used to do in the BAU and in the CTD whenever we would run into a wall. We would comb over small details looking for clues, things we might've overlooked, hoping we would get lucky. Let me ask you something… do you ever wonder if you made the right choice, working as a Fed?"

Jansen sipped her drink, considering the question. "Truthfully, I've second-guessed it a lot. We have to make a lot of tough choices and we *see* more than most people do, but I think I've helped to make a difference and that's the way you have to look at it: how you leave the world when you're gone."

The world was left no poorer once Manolo Cervantes left it, Besson thought.

"Yeah, I think you're right." he said. *What about…*

After dinner Besson and Jansen walked in Central Park, passing narrow groves, and small brooks that almost seemed musical as the water splashed on the rocks and creaked between the cracks. They both walked slowly as they passed by them, but still keeping a respectable distance from each other regardless of the narrow and private passageways.

"Did you ever find what you were looking for?" Jansen asked.

"I'm not sure yet. I think so. I hope so."

"What was wrong? — I mean, what were you missing?"

"Myself, for starters. Like I said, all I wanted to do was work for the Bureau, profiling and catching serial killers, then onto terrorists. For years, I got to do that, and it was great. I lost my job over an offense that other agents who were in better favor with all the right people would've gotten off for. The job became my life, and when I lost my job, I lost a part of myself and I didn't know where I was gonna go from there."

"The Cervantes shooting."

"Yeah," Besson replied, low and bitter.

"Is there anything you miss about the job?"

"I miss the rush I used to get, cracking the case, catching the guy, preventing an attack. I love the satisfaction I got from knowing that person won't hurt anymore people with what he was doing. Cases are like a big puzzle, and I had to put the pieces together and figure out how things fit. I learned that more times than not, if you pull the right string, the case comes loose and reveals itself. When that happens… it was great."

"It sounds like you miss more than you'd like to admit."

"I guess so, but there are things that I can do now, without worrying how my work-life would affect it. I could settle down if I want. Get a girlfriend, get married, start a family."

Jansen laughed.

"What?"

"I never thought of you as a family man," Jansen said with a smile.

"I don't know if it's something I'd go into immediately but it's something I would like to look into — maybe sooner than later considering my age — and I can do that now knowing that my job won't affect my family."

"You didn't want to do that while in the FBI?"

"It just didn't seem possible or applicable at the time."

"What do you mean?"

"Working in death and murder all the time, it's something you take home with you. It makes you edgy and unpleasant because you can't talk about it. Then, your spouse stays up late, worrying what time you come home, if you ever do, always worried when the phone rings, hoping that you won't hear the voice on the other line tell you that your wife or husband is dead. Or you, The Agent, you're in the field and you worry about your family, if you'll ever see them. Then you wonder how much danger you'd allow yourself to be in until it becomes too much."

"You have it down to a science, don't you?"

"I saw it all the time. After enough time in the BAU eventually you detach yourself from others, so when you work on the case the pain doesn't get to you; you just sift through the wreckage of humanity; the dead and the killers and the corrupt, and you just go through life as a ghost."

They walked in the park for another half hour, and double backed to where they entered.

"You know, I felt guilty," he said.

"For what?" Jansen asked.

"For pushing you away. I felt that there was something between us, and I felt bad for just pushing you away the morning I left."

She paused, then, "I couldn't help but wonder... was it something *I* did? Was there something I could've done to help you? You just up and left."

"Yeah, I left." Besson replied. His voice had a hinted guilt. "I don't think anyone could've helped me. I don't know. I just..." A heavy sigh.

After a short, but uncomfortable silence, "I'm sorry. 'I just' what?"

"Have abandonment issues."

"Yeah," Jansen replied.

"I remember," Besson said.

Jansen smiled weakly. "I don't mean to take it out on you."

"Don't worry about it — I probably had some of that coming anyway."

"Maybe a little."

Both laughed lightly.

"It's funny. Both of us lost our fathers at a young age, we were both essentially raised by our mothers, but I was the one that was fucked up."

"How is that funny?"

"…I meant in the tragic way."

"In that case, it's a fucking riot."

They both laughed, then Jansen looked back up at Besson and pushed the hair from her eye as they stared back at each other. Both of them realized what was happening and neither wanted any part of it. Besson wanted no attachments — he just wanted to focus on his mission. Jansen wanted to focus on her reshaped career.

The world around them faded into the distance: lights dimmed, sounds deafened; an embrace, and the world was different, warm.

They both drew back, shocked by the other.

"I-I'm sorry." Besson said quickly, confused and embarrassed.

"Me too,"

"This isn't something—"

"Me neither…"

"I'm sorry."

"It's not your fault. I think."

"We obviously have an unresolved issue or two."

"You're a great detective."

"What do we do now?" Besson asked.

"Well, we basically have two choices: see what happens…or not."

"You're a master of simplicity."

Besson and Jansen were kissing hard on the mouth as they went through the front door of Besson's Whitestone.

Once on his bed, still kissing, Jansen on top, she unbuckled his pants, as Besson's hands traveled under her shirt, and helped her take it off. Besson undid her bra, her breasts now bare, he massaged one, kissing and lightly biting her neck, soon moving down to the other breast, kissing and licking its perfect pink nipple. She tugged at his pants, pushing them down with her feet.

They continued to kiss, as Besson rolled her over, her back on the bed. He removed his shirt as she did her pants, and they kissed, as he maneuvered himself between her long, toned legs. She gasped as he entered her very slowly, going as far in as he could go, and tensed up—"Are you okay?"—her fingers clawed and dug into his back.

"*Don't...don't stop.*"

They continued to kiss hard, Jansen's body smelled of jasmine which aroused him further; she wrapped her legs around his waist, and her arms cradled around his neck, as their bodies bounced off one another's, sweaty and rhythmically, their heartbeats matching in pace. They explored each other, remembering how good the other tasted; the moon shining through the window, their bodies glistening, and they came together, at once, an hour later, and held each other as night crept on falling asleep, their bodies still intertwined, the entire time, laying in the warmth and light of the others hearth.

In his dreams that night, Besson, for the first time in years, walked along an uninhabited tropical beach on an island he did not know. The sun warmed and tanned his skin, as he walked along the pale white sand as the wind gently kissed his body, the entire time, watching, lost, in the gentle waves of cerulean.

The next morning, Jansen sat on the balcony in her underwear, drinking a cup of hot coffee. She wearing Besson's shirt — which was several sizes too big for her — from the night before. Besson, in pajama pants and black t-shirt, joined her with his own cup as she looked out on the city.

"Good morning."

"'Morning." Jansen looked out on the city again. "It's an incredible view."

"You get what you pay for," he replied jokingly.

Jansen faced him, and he sat next to her. "So what do we do now?" she asked.

"Well, we basically have two choices — see what happens, or not."

They embraced again, Jansen's hair fluttering around him. At once they gained a sense of acceptance that they both desired, and found in each other. Again, the world faded into the distance. There were only two people in the world at that moment, and the smell of jasmine.

9

At eight-fifteen, David Graham entered the FBI field office, and was in too much pain to notice how tired he was. A few staff members were scattered around the office, and Graham passed them by with obligatory nods. He walked into the break room where Elizabeth Tess sat alone at one of the tables, sipping a tea. Graham made some coffee, and sat with Tess awaiting percolation.

"Morning, David."

"Morning, Liz."

"Andrea phoned in a little while ago; she said she'll be in late today."

"Why?" Graham scoffed.

"She said she had family in town."

"Any news from Vegas?"

"They released Ravens, nine a.m. their time."

"Immunity?"

"Yeah."

"Son of a bitch. Is he under surveillance?"

"Yeah, they have an agent undercover on him. I thought he was going to be extradited here on conspiracy charges."

"It was all for the immunity papers. Hamlin must've signed off on it."

"There was a rumor that Langley was going to try to take Ravens if he was given to us."

Graham shook his head. "With all the heat that Langley is getting from the Manadel al-Jamadi case, the last thing anybody wants is for another terror suspect to be in *their* custody."

There was an uncomfortable silence which the television filtered out. Anderson Cooper reported: "...*with the news hitting just this morning, the Halifax corporation is withdrawing its contract with Iran. As we all know, despite sanctions, Halifax had a contract to build oil rigs in the southern region of Iran — a contract that was disclosed as being worth a number near the billions.*

"Shortly after the news broke, Halifax CEO Martin Strughold released this statement in front of reporters..."

A cut to Strughold, faded blonde hair, receding, his barrel chest wrapped in a three-thousand-dollar suit. He centered his pale blue eyes at the camera. *"It has been the decision of myself and the board of directors to dissolve our contract in Iran..."* A flurry of spitfire questions, hardly intelligible, hardly separable from the other, interrupted Strughold's testimonial. He deciphered several and answered them in a monotone, almost practiced voice. *"The sanctions did play a certain role in our ultimate decision. While the contract was worth a great deal of money, we felt as though the money would be dirty..."* — flashing a practiced smile — *"...we got the wake-up call after watching one too many episodes of* The Sopranos.*"*

Media candy — laughs all around. Questions started back up, Strughold continued, undeterred.

"By deciding to rescind the contract, we can move forward in other avenues and with other possible clients."

Reporters fired questions, which Strughold answered: *"No, there is no truth to the rumors of the dissolving of any other contracts either now or in the foreseeable future."*

A voice broke from the others. *"Mr. Strughold, is there any truth to the rumors of a weapons manufacturing contract..."*

"Those rumors hold no water..."

Tess interrupted "Bill Hamlin's office called too."

"What did they have to say?" Graham replied, vaguely disinterested.

"He had a problem with your requests. He's going to call you later today."

"Of course. My requests probably don't fit in the budget. Did his office say when?" Graham asked, limping to the coffee machine.

"They said sometime today." A beat. "When are they assigning a new SAC?"

"I'm sorry if you feel like my answering machine, but they just can't free up the money right now. We're in crisis mode and Bowman knows how to squeeze a penny. Besides, he'll probably just make Andrea SAC — legitimately — and make Dormer a lone gun brick agent. It's cheaper."

"I wouldn't mind it so much if my workload wasn't as big as it is."

"I know, but the holidays are coming up. The threat of an attack his much higher this time of year."

"It's not even mid-October."

Graham swirled the thick, sticky coffee in his cup, and fought the urge to gag as he sipped it.

"It's not even mid-October, David," Tess repeated.

"We'll have some more personnel coming within the next few months."

"God," Tess scoffed.

"Yeah."

A sudden burst of pain shot down from Graham's hip, and he clutched his cane which began to shake.

"Are you okay, David? You're turning red."

Despite the shaking of his cane, and now his leg, Graham limped over to the mirror and looked at himself. He popped two of his prescription painkillers.

"Is it your hip?"

"The coffee... the coffee, it's hot."

Graham sipped the coffee again, to wash the pills down, trying to ignore the taste. The unbearable smell started to overtake the room.

"We need a new coffee machine," Tess commented.

"Not in the budget," Graham muttered.

10

Paradise, Nevada

Wesley Hagen was sitting at a coffee booth. He stood up with his coffee, looked out onto the crowded street and watched the sun, cascading red-orange and purple in the early evening sky. He sipped the coffee slowly. He watched as Alexis Ravens ran against the traffic in the street, seemingly aimless. Hagen had been following Ravens since his release earlier that morning. His SAC was convinced that once Ravens was released, he would have a target printed on his back, which was probably true. The likelihood that Anderson would strike back at Ravens for the betrayal was exceedingly high, and judging from Ravens erratic behavior, he expected an attempt on his life shortly. Hagen slowly and casually followed Ravens across the street.

Ravens looked around him frantically, stopped to light a cigarette, check his watch, tie and retie his shoes. He changed direction at random, and sweated quite a bit.

Head down, hands in his pockets, Hagen followed with little anxiety. Hagen noticed that the only building of any relevance in the general area that Ravens tracked over again and again was a multilevel parking garage. Ravens glared at it often, fear and anger blaring from his eyes. Impatient from the wait, and no longer enjoying the incompetence of a soft target, Hagen walked toward the parking garage by himself.

After fifteen minutes of waiting, Ravens finally entered the parking garage, ignoring the attendant who told him to put out his cigarette. Hagen fiddled with his keys, pretending to open the door of a car he didn't own. Ravens quickly paced to the elevator. Hagen paused until the light blinked: BASEMENT.

Hagen ran to the attendant at the front, and flashed his badge. "Here's the number to my office. If I'm not back up here in five minutes, call the number; tell them that Agent Hagen needs backup here." Hagen then ran to the other side of the garage, to the other elevator and took it down to the basement.

Peter Lavalle leaned, relaxed, against the trunk of a car. He wore a trench coat, gloves, and sunglasses, and waited patiently for Alexis Ravens. There was a metal briefcase at his feet. "You make too much noise," Lavalle said as Ravens walked towards him. "I heard you coming the second you got off the elevator. Were you followed?"

"No, I made sure." Ravens lit another cigarette. "Do you have everything?"

Lavalle motioned to the briefcase at his feet. Ravens snatched it and opened it on the trunk of the car.

"That's it? Ten thousand dollars?"

"Be happy you got that much, along with the new passport."

"Passport? The papers I signed said I can't leave the country."

"I don't want you in this country anymore."

"I'll need a car to get to the airport,"

Lavalle knocked on the trunk. "Right here," he said, handing Ravens the keys. "There should be a plane ticket in the case also. I think I gave you quite a bit, actually."

Quietly, Hagen crouched under a car, within ear shot of the two men. He stared at both of them through the car window, keeping his head as low as possible. He was only able to get a profile view of the man with Ravens; from the angle he was watching them.

"Can't leave the country, eh? Couldn't you have cut a better deal with the Bureau? They didn't even give you a way out. Not a plane ticket, not a car, not any money... what happened to all of your money, anyway?"

"Immunity was all I could get, they said I was lucky."

"Aren't we all?"

Ravens lit another cigarette.

"Slow down," Lavalle warned.

"Listen, Peter, I'm sorry. I really am, but I had to cover my own ass."

"*Peter...*" Hagen whispered to himself.

"I understand; you had to save *your* business even if it meant endangering *mine.*"

"And I didn't know Anderson was working with *you.*"

"Had you known, would it have made of a difference?"

Ravens took a long pull of his cigarette and looked away.

"I thought not." Lavalle readied himself to leave. "Now remember: I am to *never* see you again."

Ravens watched Lavalle as he was walking away. "Thank you," he said, exasperated.

"Leave."

Slowly, and silently, Hagen moved closer, taking his gun from its holster. Under what seemed to be Ravens car, there was a blinking red light emitting from a metallic box.

Ravens entered the car as Hagen stood and yelled "Stop!" But the key turned, the car started. Hagen's desperate wail had been smothered by the backlash from the blast, which shattered the windows, deflated the tires, and sounded off the alarms of all the cars in the area. Hagen only saw a bright light, and suddenly found himself several feet back from where he was, immobile, bleeding from his nose and ears. His eyelids fluttered, and couldn't feel his legs shaking before he entered shock.

Now on the main floor, Peter Lavalle ran towards the entrance as the attendant, who had called Hagen's office, ran towards him. Lavalle heard the sound of sirens blaring, coming closer by the second. He pulled a .45 caliber Colt Officer's Model with ivory grips, fired twice, and the attendant fell dead on the ground. He fired a few shots to the DVD players recording the feed from the cameras, as well as destroying the DVDs inside them.

A panel truck stopped in front of the entrance and Lavalle jumped in — all before the authorities arrived.

11

Manhattan, New York

"There's another wrinkle," Jansen said to the rest of the conference room. "Our sources in the media are saying there's going to be a story about the tightened security. They're going to suggest that there's a terrorist threat that the public is being kept in the dark on."

"When?" Graham asked.

"As early as this evening's news."

"Jesus. If we do come out with the possibility of a terrorist attack, how do you think the public will react?"

"Hard to say. There will be at least *some* unrest."

"How much?"

"Manageable. These sorts of vague threats come up in the media often enough."

Eventually people are stripped of their humanity, and become nothing more than statistics on a screen. Jansen watched it happening now.

"If we come out about it now, it will impede the investigation. If we come out with it *after* we stop the threat it can be looked at in two ways: either we saved the day or we didn't alert the public that a terrorist organization had plans to hit us hard and we rolled the dice with American lives," Dormer argued.

"Every time a crisis is averted the press always goes nuts about the information we withheld," he continued. "It's going to happen anyway, so right now let them come out with the story. Tomorrow, after it becomes public, we'll release a statement saying its all part of a training method, or some experimental new security directive, or some shit like that. Don, that's your world, make it your priority."

"What happens when the press actually finds out about the threat, after the investigation is complete?" Walker asked.

"Well, if we successfully intercept the terrorists and stop the attack, in that case, say that we received a tip from an informant saying that there was going to be an attempt within twelve or twenty-four hours, and we had to react quickly."

A staffer quickly walked into the conference room.

"Yes?" Graham asked, annoyed.

"Sir, Vegas just gave us a report. Alexis Ravens is dead."

12

Among the many perks of being the CEO of a highly successful enterprise, having his private jet was one of his favorites. A glass of brandy in his hand, Strughold looked out into the colorful sunset, and became quickly bored by its cheap display. In front of him was a conference phone, and he dialed two numbers. Besson and Lavalle answered their respective lines.

"Well, gents, what do you have for me?" Strughold asked.

"Anderson is on board," Lavalle reported. "He is still a little rough on the edges but when he heard about the Pentagon he started cooperating."

"Is his attitude going to be a problem?"

"He's just being bold in front of his people," Besson said.

"Ahh, the touchstone of any good leader." Strughold laughed. "Does he suspect he's being used?"

"Not a clue."

Another laugh. "Good. Is everything quiet on your side of the world, Will?"

"Not even a whisper. The Washington Bureau's put all of its resources into their investigation into the motorcade incident, and from the looks of things they don't have much to go on.

"However, each major office is at an elevated threat level, and so far the Bureau and the military have been surprisingly good at keeping this matter quiet."

"In your approximation, how close do you think they're going to get?" Lavalle asked.

"We'll be at a comfortable distance. They're probably going to keep their focus on DC, considering its proximity to the extraction site. We won't have any trouble until we try to ship. Where is the bomb now?"

"We set up a containment area in a warehouse in the Virginia slums," Lavalle said.

"Be careful: satellite scans might pick up the radiological output," Besson said.

"We have heeded your advice. We lined the walls with granite, as you suggested."

"In what condition is the bomb now?" Besson asked.

"I'll put Moira on the line; she can explain it better than I."

Lavalle's end was silent for a time.

Finally, the silence was broken. "As far as I can see the bomb is in perfect condition," Dr. Grey reported. "However, there is something you should all know. The bomb, while nuclear, is a hydrogen model."

They all knew what it meant; a higher capacity, a stronger yield. More dangerous, but more powerful.

"Will it be a problem?" Lavalle asked.

"My proclivity is to nuclear devices, their models make no difference."

"Good."

"It will take some time, but it will be ready to be dropped soon."

"That could be a problem, actually," Besson said. "Due to the target area, an air attack is far out of the question; do you think you can modify the bomb to have it detonate from inside a building, let's say?"

"That... would be complicated, but it can be done. There might be fewer casualties because it will be detonated from the ground, but since it will be in the winter with likely high winds and the fact that this bomb's yield is several kilotons greater than our original projections I'd say everything should be fine."

"How long?" Strughold asked.

"Weeks."

"Fine."

"Do you want it set for a countdown or by remote detonation?" Dr. Grey asked.

"Both."

"How close must you be to detonate it by remote, if need be?" Besson asked.

"Even if you were out of the state, it will still go through. I could fix a PDA to work like that."

"Alright."

"I can design a keypad that could control the bomb totally — activate or deactivate, detonate on command; monitor or change the countdown sequence."

"How long will it take to design, build and connect it to the main circuit board of the bomb?"

"Add two weeks to the time it will take for me to do the original modifications."

"Can you wait?" Strughold asked.

"I have time," Besson replied with indifference.

"The keypad isn't a good idea," Lavalle said after a short silence. Having every aspect of that bomb controlled in *one* device and held by *one* man poses too great a risk. It might sound diminutive but I'd rather be safe than sorry."

"In case the bomb is tampered by an outsider or Will is on the verge of capture, the PDA could be used," Strughold said.

"And what if Will isn't unaware the bomb is being tampered with?"

"Thank you for the vote of confidence," Besson muttered.

"I can tamperproof it," Dr. Grey insisted, "have it immediately detonate if any of the circuits are severed or if any pertinent hardware is removed."

"Happy?" Besson asked dryly.

"Are you sure your transportation idea won't get the bomb detected?" Lavalle said.

"The ports have radiation scanners, and it's far from foolproof," Besson replied. "If we contain it properly it will slip through. We could contain it in granite or a lead casing. The only way the Radiological Assistance Program or the Search Response Teams would get involved is if somebody actually scans the container, actually looking for something directly."

All open ports in America had radiological scanners that were installed by the Department of Homeland Security to detect nuclear radiation. They were far from perfect, and easily deceived.

The Radiological Assistance Program and the Search Response Team are parts of the Department of Energy that specialize in the finding and assessing of radiological materials, specifically of a nuclear nature. They are run by the Nuclear Emergency Support Team (NEST), and they are the best at what they do. However, the FBI is largely in command of any response in the matter, and can decide whether to deploy NEST and its branches or not — that is, of course, if they were focusing on that particular area.

Besson, a former FBI agent, knew how to avoid such attention, not that it would be that hard anyway.

"Are we all on the same page now?" Strughold asked. Everyone agreed. "I suggest we have one of these every week until the inevitable."

"Not quite a meeting of the five families, but it's doable," Besson said. "Where will the rest of you be?"

"Splitting my time between Virginia and Nevada until the Anderson matter is finished," Lavalle said.

"I'll be in Manhattan for the duration," Besson said.

"I'll be back in New York within a month. I have appearances to make and business to take care of," Strughold said. "Make sure my house is in order."

It was during Strughold's last statement, before the four adjourned and went on their ways, Besson noticed, that even now Strughold was like the director of an orchestra in an opera, making sure that each note was played to perfection. He was a consummate businessman, or perhaps a taxidermist for that matter.

Now, as if he were directing the opera, Besson considered who to cast in the next act.

13

On the main floor, Elizabeth Tess looked over the report regarding the Ravens assassination from Vegas. Graham and Jansen stood by her side. "Ravens was in a parking garage. The car he was in had a bomb in it, which detonated when he started it. Their forensic teams also suspect he met with someone just before he was killed, and it was that person who planted the bomb in the first place."

"What evidence do they have to support that?" Graham asked.

"A security guard was found shot in the head near the entrance. The way his body was found, it seemed that he was running toward either the elevator or the person who shot him."

"Do you think it was Anderson?" Graham asked.

"I wouldn't be surprised one bit," Jansen replied. "Liz, what happened to the agent that was tailing Ravens?"

"He was caught in the blast."

"Is he alive?" Graham asked.

"It doesn't say."

Walker slammed his phone back on the receiver. "Vegas just reported that their agent, Wesley Hagen, is in surgery right now. He was found in deep shock, with two shattered ribs, a severe concussion, internal bleeding and a possible spinal cord injury."

"Will he live?" Graham asked.

"Don't know yet. They said they'll keep us apprised."

"David," Dormer called. "I just got off the phone with Bill Hamlin. He wants us to send over all of our information on the C-4, the investigation, Ravens and Josh Anderson."

"Why?"

"He's flying to Vegas in an hour to help with the investigation on their end. A goodwill thing."

"Don, I want you on that flight!"

"What?"

"You heard me. Pack your things and head over to the Quantico office to meet him."

"That's like a three hour drive!"

"I'll have a helicopter pick you up on the roof. Jim, get back on the phone with Hamlin and patch him through to my office."

"You got it."

"Wait, David — what about my workload?" Walker asked.

"Split it among the techs and interns."

"When am I coming back?"

"When Hamlin and I say so." Then to Jansen he said, "Andrea, you and Jim hit the streets. Liz, print out the top ten names on the NCTC list for New York and give it to Andrea. Rattle some cages, see who squawks."

As he finished his shower, Will Besson received a call on his cell phone. He picked it up off the sink and checked the ID. If it had been a restricted number, he knew it would be Lavalle. It was Andrea Jansen instead. Besson was somewhat relieved — it had been two days since their date.

"Hey, Will."

"Hey, how's it going?"

"Not too bad, I'm in the field right now. What about you?"

"In the nude."

"Caught you in the shower?"

"No, I was just with one of my other girlfriends."

"Smartass."

"Always."

"That's a real shame; I was going to ask you if you were free tonight, but now I guess I'll have to call one of *my* other *boy*friends."

"Well I hope they're all busy," Besson replied.

"Why, are all of your *girl*friends busy?"

"They are, actually."

"That's good. So I guess you're free tonight."

"Yep."

"Great. Any ideas?"

Besson took a long moment. The city was on borrowed time, and before its time expired, Besson had unfinished personal matters to attend to besides that of the bomb.

"Are you still alive, Will?"

"Yeah, I'm here."

"Do you have any ideas for tonight?" Jansen repeated.

"I think so."

"Would you mind filling me in? Not all of us are detectives, you know."

"Lindy's. It's a restaurant by MSG."

"I've heard of it."

"What time do you want to meet?" Besson asked.

"I'm not sure yet, I'll let you know."

"Great, call me."

"I will. Talk to you then."

"Great. Bye."

"Bye."

The steam in the bathroom had slowly dwindled and then totally disappeared. Besson stared at himself in the mirror. The hot water from his shower had turned his body a light shade of red. Looking down at his side, he saw the discoloration of a brown scar, five inches across, compliments of the late Manolo Cervantes, on his right hip. It never colored or tanned, and it never healed. Suddenly stung with a fleeting sense of shame, Besson tied a towel around his waist, making sure the scar was covered. He dried himself with another towel and attempted to collect his thoughts. He had to focus. Tonight a childhood demon had to be faced — and hopefully bested. Besson knew of no other way to gain closure on the matter of his family. At this juncture in his life, the angst and troubles he lived through as a child shouldn't be at the forefront of his mind, however it lingered. It demanded attention and finality. After so many years of running from it, Besson decided to oblige.

Later, he sat on his balcony and quietly gazed at the city in front of him. As if a temporary amnesia had stricken him and he had only now come out, Besson remembered the reason he had returned to New York. He questioned himself as to why he still wanted to see her, and questioned the logic of that want. Truly, he wanted her beyond the realms of sex or information; he cared about her genuinely, but was unsure what to do with her when he considered his mission. She simply didn't fit into the plan.

Besson considered the possibilities for hours, weighing them with the consequences, and came to no conclusion. In his bedroom, he lay down on his bed and tried to relax. His muscles were tense and his head throbbed. He listened to the rhythm of his heartbeat, and could hear the sound the bomb would make upon detonation. Through the bed sheets, a tingeing smell of jasmine teased his nostrils. An impossible suggestion crossed Besson's mind, and quickly departed. He could see in Jansen a different life: a small wedding, a house in a docile and sleepy suburb, holiday dinners, anniversaries spent sipping wine by the fireplace, a white-picket fence, a dog, Fourth of July barbeques, first days of school, watching the kids open gifts early on Christmas mornings, birthday parties, little league games, parent-teacher conferences, sunsets, grandkids, a fitting death from old age surrounded by loved ones, snowy winters and warm summers, a slower-paced life.

Besson showered again. He felt the need to apologize to her, but he didn't know why.

From outside the interrogation room, Jansen watched Graham through the one-way mirror as he grilled one of the NCTC list suspects that Jansen and Dormer had detained.

The interrogation room was a dull and dreary gray, and complimented the color of the sky coming through the large window facing Gibson's back. For several seconds, Graham looked out the window through sleepless eyes.

Dormer joined Jansen with the suspects file. "Vernon Gibson, age thirty-five with a sheet a mile long, has done time mostly in South America."

"Is he an immigrant?"

"Nope; born and raised in the good ol' U-S-of-A. He just pulled shit on the other side of the border before setting up shop here in 2002."

"What charges did he face in South America?"

"Narcotics and smuggling. He flipped on his buddies and ended up doing four years of a twenty-odd year sentence."

In the interrogation room, Graham paced around Gibson, purposely stomping his cane hard on the floor with each step. Gibson jumped almost every time.

"He looks about ready to boil," Dormer observed.

"Yeah."

"So what are you going to tell me?" Graham suddenly boomed.

Gibson almost squealed, "I don't know what you're talking about!"

"Listen, I've been doing this longer than you've been alive. That means I've been lied to by all kinds of losers and shit bags. I've seen great liars and bad ones. And son, you're a terrible fucking liar!"

Gibson's shaking became apparent to Jansen and Dormer, as opposed to just Graham. He didn't say anything.

"Okay then, Vernon. I'll tell *you* a few things first. Your main source of income comes from smuggling and drugs. Recently you've been getting calls from a woman with an accent, probably English. This woman has promised you money if you do some favors for her."

"Y-you tapped my phone?"

"That's right, you little shit. You see, that's what happens to people that do illegal things in this country. They're found, they're prosecuted, and they spend the rest of their useless lives — such as yours — in prison." Graham slammed his hand on the table which made Gibson jump again. "Hammer just fell on you, son. So whatcha got for me?"

Gibson, still shaking and nervous, seemed to be weighing his options. He cleared his throat and asked, "Wh-what's in it for me?"

"We can talk your sentence down if you give us some good evidence that leads to an arrest or the derailing of a terrorist attack. *Years* can be shaved off of your sentence."

"I want immunity."

"Get real, there's no chance. If I were you, I'd take what I could get."

"I want immunity!" Gibson repeated.

"Okay, fine. So we'll put you away on charges of aiding and protecting terrorists, which translates also into a charge of treason. Treason in and of itself is twenty-five years to life, if you escape the needle. Now, we can get you immunity from being prosecuted for treason, but the rest of the charges will stand. We'll tell the judge that you were helpful, you might get some leniency."

Gibson said nothing.

"I hope you like Guantanamo," Graham said. He turned and was heading for the door when Gibson called back to him. Graham looked up to the one-way, with a slight smirk and a wink.

"Son of a bitch," Jansen said, impressed by Graham's tactics.

"That old prick's still got it," Dormer replied.

"What do you have for me, my boy?" Graham asked.

"What do you want?"

"My hip back..."

"And the Oscar goes to..." Jansen muttered.

"...but I'll settle for information. Like the name of the woman you've been talking to, the details of the plan she kept alluding to, and any other bits of information we could use. Keep in mind, kiddo, the more you give, the more years we take off your sentence."

Gibson was hesitating.

Graham said in a low voice, "You look a little bit thin, Vernon. A little pasty. If I were to make you take a drug test, how do you think you'd do? If we find drugs in your place that's a felony possession beef. Jesus Christ, by the time you get out, you'll probably be my age."

"I-I-I don't know her name."

"What did she tell you?"

"She told me that this guy was going to offer me money for services, that he'd ask about renting some trucks to, like, move shit or something. She was like a middleman. He did and I got him the trucks."

"Did she tell you the guy's name?"

"Something with an A."

"Anderson? Was it Josh Anderson?"

"Yeah... probably."

"It's a yes or no question. So *yes* or *no*?"

"Yes, yes." He was whining, spittle coming through his lips, down his chin.

"Good."

"Am I finished?"

"Not by a long shot. Do you know what the trucks are supposed to be used for?"

"She said it was for a terrorist attack,"

"You're a piece of shit. Did Anderson find you?"

"Yeah."

"This kid would name the pope if he could," Dormer muttered.

Graham's cell phone went off. He spoke with the person on the other line briefly, then quickly limped out of the room.

"I have to run an errand. Andrea, you're in charge. Finish debriefing him, make sure he tells you everything. I'll be on my cell."

"David..."

"I did all the hard stuff already, just finish it."

"I don't want to go to prison!" Gibson screamed.

Graham scoffed at Gibson from the one-way, and as quickly as he could, he limped away, leaving the office.

"I don't want to go to prison!"

"Jesus Christ," Dormer muttered. "Should I go or should you?"

Gibson began to weep.

"Can you?" Jansen asked.

"I really don't want to."

"This is a matter of national security."

"Yeah..."

Gibson wet his pants.

"Shit," Jansen muttered.

"You mean piss."

"Go in there, Jim."

"Come on, Andrea."

"I'm the ranking officer."

"That's right, *you* are."

"Rock, Paper, Scissor?"

"Okay."

Jansen: rock; Dormer: paper.

"Damnit."

"Have fun."

"Stay right here," Jansen ordered.

The interrogation room smelled of urine, but it didn't seem to bother Gibson, whose weeping was beginning to subside. Jansen cringed when she entered the room and stood as far from the puddle as she could.

"I don't want to go to prison!"

"Shutup. You just told my superior that the trucks were going to be used in a terrorist attack. Did Josh Anderson show up for the trucks?"

"Yeah."

"Okay, how many people were with him?"

"A couple others."

"And they took two trucks, I'm assuming."

"Yeah."

"What kind of trucks?"

"Dump trucks, they said they were transporting some sort of explosive."

"C-4?"

"I don't know." A pleading sob.

"Do you know when or where they're planning on using it?"

"They said they needed a map to the Manhattan Bridge."

"Jim," Jansen called. "Get in touch with Quantico and tell them. Tell Tess that I need Mr. Gibson's office bugged and his calls routed here." To Gibson she said, "Do you have the license plates of the trucks?"

"Yeah, at my office."

"Jim, go pick those things up, and get Mr. Gibson a clean pair of pants."

"What about my deal?" Gibson asked.

"You'll have to talk to Mr. Graham about that."

"Well, where did he go?"

"No idea." Then to Dormer, "Oh, and Jim?"

From the one-way, "Yeah."

"Get the goddamn janitor."

14

Besson and Jansen met outside of Lindy's and walked in together. Jansen didn't notice that Besson took a deep breath and held it as they entered. Besson noticed that the maître d' at the greeting desk was different from the one he had encountered weeks prior. He felt relieved, even though it didn't really matter.

"Just two?" asked the maître d'.

"Yes," Jansen replied.

To Besson's shock, they were seated at the same booth his family and he were seated at over twenty-five years ago. He swallowed hard and hesitated before he followed. Jansen took the first seat, and Besson took the one across from her, and sat exactly where his father had sat. He stirred momentarily.

"A waitress will come by to take your order." The maître d' said.

"Are you okay, Will? You look a little flushed."

"Yeah, fine."

Jansen hesitated for a moment, uncomfortable with what she wanted to say. She sipped her water and said, "I know we haven't really talked much since... I'm mean the last time we saw each other was at your place..."

Besson was a little confused. "Yeah..."

"I was wondering if you still feel the same way. You said you still wanted to... and I just wanted to know if you changed your mind. If it was just a heat of the moment thing."

"It wasn't the heat of the moment. I still feel the same way I did before."

"Are you sure?"

"I wouldn't be here if I didn't want to be, if I felt any different."

"I'm sorry, I was just... wondering."

"Are *you* sure?"

Jansen smiled. "I think so."

Besson wiped the sweat from his forehead with his napkin, and drank most of the water in the glass in front of him.

"Are you okay?" Jansen asked.

"I'm on the jones."

"Really? What are you using?"

"Methadone for a while, then I reverted back to smack."

"I'm impressed. You've kept your weight up."

Both chuckled lightly.

The waitress brought over two menus and a complementary basket of bread. Jansen ordered a diet coke; Besson a shot of Bacardi 151 and a Rolling Rock.

"It's just... I've been here before."

"Uh-huh," Jansen said, confused.

Besson quickly downed the shot and chugged a quarter of his beer.

"Hey, slow down a little."

"I just need to compose myself a little."

"What's wrong?"

After a long gulp of his beer Besson looked stiffly and tiredly at Jansen. He wavered, sighed and recounted the Lindy's story from his youth. With every word from his detailed description the surroundings melted away, and under it the old form of the restaurant took shape. Christmas decorations were up, dirty snow was on the ground outside, and the temperature dropped twenty degrees. He told the story through older eyes, but with the details only a child would remember.

Five minutes later, the past again receded; the restaurant retook its present form, the weather outside changed back, Besson was no longer a child sitting across from his parents. It was again the present, and he was sitting in the same seat his father had. The reminder made him stir again. Besson had finished his story, and he slumped slightly, lowered his head and stuffed a piece of bread in his mouth to cover his waning voice. He did not tear, nor did he sob. He didn't know how to anymore.

Taken aback by the sudden revelation, it took Jansen several seconds to react. She eventually did, placing her hand on his and telling him that everything was okay. As he told her the story he looked as if he had relived it, his eyes seemed to have changed; they were darker, narrower. Jansen remembered how alike they were. Their feelings had been bottled up for so long, and their childhoods had shaped them into who they were and why they led the lives they did.

They both secretly hoped that the more they distanced themselves from their pasts the sooner they would come to think what happened was the memories of someone else, in some other life.

"I didn't know, Will. I'm so sorry."

Besson cleared his throat. He seemed to have calmed down somewhat.

"It's not your fault. It explains my behavior tonight. I'm sorry if I upset you."

"Why did you want to come here then?"

"Because I have to face this place."

"Does the drinking help at all?" Jansen asked, somewhat unconvinced.

"Am I drinking because I'm upset, or am I upset because I'm drinking?" Besson mused with a light laugh.

Besson's laugh calmed Jansen down — he wasn't so on edge anymore.

"That reminds me of this movie, *Leaving Las Vegas*."

"Never seen it."

"It's about a career alcoholic who goes to Vegas to drink himself to death. Nick Cage was in it."

"I'll take a wild guess and say it wasn't a comedy."

"No, it was really depressing actually."

"And I remind you of a career alcoholic?" Besson said with a smile.

"No, no, no. Just that thing you said. In the movie Nick Cage says something like: 'Do I drink because my wife left me, or did my wife leave me because I drink?' What you said just reminded me of it."

"You know, I never liked Nicolas Cage."

"Still, you should check the movie out, it's really good. I think it's up your alley."

"Maybe I will."

"But, I'll remind you of this one thing, just to keep in mind," — a wink — "'the man takes a drink, the drink takes a drink, then the drink takes the man'."

Besson, in the middle of a swill, brought the glass just close enough to his mouth to purse his bottom lip on the rim and wryly muttered, "Fuck you."

Jansen laughed. "Always with the quick comebacks."

"At least that's the only thing about me that's quick."

"I think you're losing your sarcastic edge in your old age," Jansen said.

"I'm just a little rusty. Haven't sparred with you in a while."

"Same here."

"I missed your sense of humor," Besson said.

"Well, it's your humor — you're a bad influence — so you only missed yourself."

A smirk. "I still haven't found me."

She smiled.

"Is work any better?" he asked.

"It is what it is, I'm used to the way things are."

"I told you — eventually you learn to just turn it off and live with it."

"I guess you were right."

"I think I'm a little wise beyond my years," Besson said with a smirk.

"Don't forget modest."

"That too."

They laughed, more relaxed suddenly.

"When did you learn to turn it off?" she asked.

"I never learned to turn if off totally, but it worked most of the times."

"When would it come back on?"

"I'd say the worst example would have to be Manolo Cervantes. But before that, the case that had allowed me to initially turn it off was a case I had around my third or fourth year in the BAU, when we were tracking this serial rapist. Section Chief Sullivan came up with a plan, and in a meeting he asked if I agreed with him because I was his yes-man. I said no. I had a different plan he didn't approve of, and he stuck to his idea. I went to the AD, and he agreed with me and we caught him.

"What we didn't know was that the rapist evolved into a kidnapper. He took two girls that he kept in his house as chew toys. When we found them one was dead; the other one was hanging on by a thread. She slipped into a coma and never woke up. Had Sullivan and I not fought over tactics we would've found them in time. After that... everything just passed in a blur. Cases became words on a paper, and I learned to live with it."

"That sounds horrible."

"Yeah."

Besson didn't tell her that he and Carl McDowell were the ones who had discovered the two kidnapped girls. They were the UNSUB's neighbor's children. Fifteen and eighteen, found chained up in the basement, gagged. The fifteen-year-old had been orally raped, beaten, and fornicated with a wrench which hadn't been removed. The eighteen year old was sodomized and strangled. Besson's profile had been correct. More often than not, the rapist couldn't maintain an erection.

In actuality, both victims survived. The eighteen year old, in the years that followed, went down a slope of drugs and prostitution, until she overdosed after snorting four bags of tainted of heroin. The fifteen-year-old had trouble walking and committed suicide shortly after her sister's overdose.

Besson thought about that morning, gray and dreary, and his face suddenly looked long and sad; his eyes lost in the past.

Not realizing what had been troubling him, not totally wrong, Jansen asked, "That... ordeal... with your parents, before they... the way it affected you..."

"Yeah, it did, but as I got older, and I matured, it stopped affecting my life and I was able to move on. It still bothers me sometimes — especially when I used to deal with child abuse cases. Those cases hurt me the most. My biggest fear was — and still is — seeing other kids growing up the way I did... or worse, having kids and seeing them grow up the way I did."

"It still bothers you?"

"Does it bother *you*? You know about this kind of thing as much me."

"The pain doesn't go away, really."

"And it'll never get easier, you know it, and you live with it."

"We've had to learn to live with a lot of things haven't we?"

"Yeah,"

There was a sad silence that Besson broke after a minute.

"I'm sorry."

"For what?"

"Being such a buzz-kill."

After finishing dinner, Besson stared off, looking around the restaurant. He wasn't dazed as he was earlier, he was alert — and he seemed to be taking the restaurant in, as if he had just now walked in for the first time.

"Are you okay?" Jansen asked.

"Getting there."

"You know, I spent all my life running from what happened, trying to forget it. We both went through some shit. With all that pain, why don't you try to forget it and walk away?"

Besson thought it over for a time. "Because it's mine."

Later, Jansen brought Besson back to her apartment just off of Union Square Park. The apartment was simple and uncluttered, the archetype of docility. Jansen kept very few personal possessions, except for a picture of her mother, pale and thin, which sat on the coffee table. It was a modest apartment, small and compact. The kitchen was to the right as you walked in, the living room was straight ahead, bathroom in the back and just right of the living room was the small, single bedroom.

"Try not to get too excited while you're here."

"In this funhouse? How could I contain myself?" Besson remarked.

"I didn't take much from my mom — I wanted to do things on my own."

"Considering we both live in Manhattan I thought we would have to compare our places. But I think we're tied for Most Boring."

"You right. Since we live in the city we should have extravagant things, right?"

"I think so."

"Well then, to Park Avenue!"

"I'll call the limo driver."

Besson and Jansen, exhausted from the exchange, sat tiredly on the living room couch. Besson ached. Jansen draped her legs over Besson's as she sat horizontally on the couch, her back on the armrest. Besson rubbed her legs, firm, and smooth, slowly up and down as she made eights on the nape of Besson's neck with her index finger.

Their heartbeats slowed, a stare, their heartbeats paced faster, and held each other afterward.

15

Washington, D.C.

Security at the Pentagon was intensive and repetitive. It took forty minutes for Strughold to get through it and the armed guard that escorted him to his destination took another seven.

The guard brought him to enclosed double doors. He slid a keycard to unlock it.

"Thank you," Strughold said.

The soldier remained stoic. "I'll be waiting outside."

"Right."

Strughold entered slowly, a round table taking up the vast circumference of the room. The Joint Chiefs sat in front of him, as stoic as the guard had been.

Chairman of the Joint Chiefs Richard Stapleton greeted him with a handshake that could've easily crushed his hand. The idea was not at all that surprising to Strughold, Stapleton being a man of war-hardened metal. Moreover, the men still seated were all of the same proliferation, which, underneath his veneer of calm coordination, made Strughold increasingly nervous. Being an imposing man himself, Strughold was habituated as being the most commanding and intimidating man in the room, though here, he was on the same level as these men of stone, if not beneath them. It was emasculating.

Strughold knew, however, not to let on that he was intimidated, knowing that these soldiers were attuned to smell even the thinnest sense of fear.

Strughold steeled himself.

"Mr. Strughold," Stapleton greeted. "Please, sit."

Strughold sat facing the imperturbable congregation of the most powerful military officials in the country. If Strughold betrayed any sign of fear it was not picked up.

"Good morning, gentlemen." Placing his stuffed leather suitcase on the table, he opened it up and passed out copies of manila envelopes to the congregation.

One of the faceless gargoyles said, "Is this your proposal?"

"Indeed."

As they mulled over the files handed out to them, Strughold narrated. "This is but a tip of what we at Halifax can do for you."

A murmur off somewhere: "With the funding."

"You have to spend money to make money in this world. I'm sure you've heard that before," Strughold said, hitting an early stride.

"How much will this put us back?"

"Does the security of this country have a price tag on it?" Strughold mused.

The air in the room was heavier. These were not the men to make light of their commitment to their country.

"Let's say there was interest in the areas suggested in this file, when would we begin to see results?" Stapleton asked.

"As you know these projects will take years to cultivate until..."

"The gestation period then."

Strughold fought a smile. "We can have prototypes ready within a few months." He let the answer sink in. "Have I piqued your interests?"

The room was beginning to burst, and Strughold was ready to push forward.

"In these days when 9/11 is quickly becoming a distant memory and people are feeling much less afraid then they were even two years ago — especially now that the tragedy is being relegated to films that aren't nominated because it's still too morbid — the funding of military tech is dwindling." Once the 9/11 card is played most people took its side, rather than seem apathetic. The men were interested now. Strughold mused that this was how the second Iraq war broke out. "By using Halifax as a resource, you're keeping your interests inside our country's borders and a little more cost effective. By accepting this offer, you will not only ensure the safety of this country and our troops but also create profound dents in the armor of this nation's enemies.

"We used to be a superpower. We can return to that former glory. Rome isn't burning just yet."

The room was his, the stone faces were acquiescent, fitting to form exactly as Strughold intended. He looked upon his audience then, no more than a few generations past warlords, divvying up the small world they knew between their number.

"This proposal of yours still needs to be passed up the ladder. The SecDef in particular. Frankly I don't know how well this kind of thing will go over with him — a sleeping-with-the-enemy sort of thing."

"I'm far from the enemy."

"You were in bed with Iran," said a general.

"Operative word being *were*," Strughold spat. "My company is far from treasonous and my intentions are only patriotic in derivation. I hope you will look at my proposal from that angle, and leave the past where it remains."

"You know we'd like nothing more than to jump on this," Stapleton said. "But we need to follow protocol." He waved the file. "This will just collect dust if we don't move on it now."

A satisfied smile. "I wholeheartedly agree."

16

Manhattan, New York

Andrea Jansen stepped off the elevator and walked into the FBI's CT floor the next morning, and as always, Dormer met her with two coffees.

"Did they fix the machine yet?" Jansen asked.

"No."

"Keep it. Any leads?"

"We're looking for the trucks from the description Gibson gave us and we're trying to match the plate numbers, but we haven't found any of them."

"Is he bullshitting?"

"No. The DMV corroborates that the plates are real, so those trucks are out there. We also tapped his lines and directed all calls here."

"Is he expecting any more calls from these people?"

"He said their payment plan was half now, half later. He also asked to be told when the attack would go down so he could avoid using the bridge that day."

"He's not so dumb after all."

"Yeah, right."

"What does David have to say about all this?"

"Beats the shit out of me."

"What?"

"Called in a few minutes ago. He sounded like shit, said he wasn't gonna come in till later, if at all."

Jansen and Dormer walked up to Tess, who was at her desk.

"If we can't find those trucks, it probably means they're being kept somewhere out of the way. What are some available places in the area that could house them?"

"Any place that could fit them," Dormer muttered.

"I'll call the Sanitation Department and ask if they've seen any strange vehicles in their yards," Tess said.

"Anything from the desert?"

"Don faxed a report to us late last night from Vegas."

"What did it say?"

"The Vegas agent that was found in the garage after the explosion has been questioned and he only remembers bits and pieces of what happened."

"Anything relevant?"

"No."

"Were there any video cameras taping the downstairs lot?" Dormer asked.

"There were, but they were hit in the explosion. The DVD records were destroyed by gunshots too."

"Did the Vegas forensic unit take a look at the bomb that was used on the car?" Jansen asked.

"Yeah, they confirmed that it was the same type that Ravens sold to Josh Anderson."

Dormer chuckled. "Love that irony."

"Any luck finding Anderson?"

"Nothing yet," Dormer reported. "Our best link is still Gibson."

"Where is he?"

"He's at his office," Dormer replied. "Agents are with him in his apartment and a few lookouts are in the area."

"Let's go see how he's doing."

The office in which Vernon Gibson conducted his business was a small basement area, behind a metal door in a narrow, dark alley. It was out of the way and hardly noticeable — perfect for a man who wishes to carry out an illicit business. The walk down the stairs was dark, and pipes dripped around them. Dormer started to whistle the theme from the *Halloween* movies.

Past another door and down a hallway, which was just as musty and dark and with the same problematic plumbing, was the small office. It was surprisingly bright, with a desk, a phone, a laptop, and a cabinet where Gibson kept a shotgun. Gibson's bodyguard, a large, imposing man, sat handcuffed to a chair at the other side of the room. Four FBI agents, their ties hanging over their Kevlar vests, watched Gibson, who had been staring at the phone for hours. The phone had wires coming out of the receiver, which were connected to earpieces making it possible for others to listen to his conversations. At the office, Elizabeth Tess had flooded the frequency on Gibson's phone so all calls would be routed through to the FBI's network, and could be traced from there.

Gibson, a fairly young man, seemed to have aged years in the few days since his arrest. He had not shaved, had eaten very little and slept only when given direct consent. His thick-necked assistant, Warren Ragucci, was seated near him. Ragucci was arrested for aiding and abetting, and was likely to flip to avoid sentencing.

"Has Mr. Gibson received any phone calls yet?" Jansen asked.

"Yeah, but none were from Anderson or the woman who originally contacted him," an agent told her.

"Anything juicy?"

"We had him pretend everything was business as usual. We're gonna have a field day with this. Four calls, all of them were NCTC list names. Local and federal teams are en route to their locations as we speak?"

"Are we getting the collars?"

"We have the evidence."

"But no Anderson…"

"That's right."

"The glass is always half empty," Dormer replied.

"Were you given a timetable when they were supposed to get in contact with you?" Jansen asked Gibson. "Or at least an estimate when to stop running shipments?"

"No, nothing."

"You jerking us off, Vernon?"

As Jansen predicted, Vernon became flustered when she said that to him. It's always different when a woman says something pertaining to sex, especially so graphically. This was a rare moment in which Jansen relished the double standard of men and women.

"They told me to stay by the phone, that they'd call," Vernon persisted. "They said they liked the way I did business and they would tell me when to stop running shipments across the bridge as a professional courtesy. They said that if this worked out, we'd do business again."

"Once the attack succeeds and thousands of people are killed," Dormer added.

Gibson shrugged. "They pay good."

"You know, it's people like you who'd jump on anything that comes along that makes the seven year itch so popular," Jansen said.

The damp basement fell into a sullen silence. Far away, into the dark, distant hallway, the sound of a dripping pipe could be heard. Gibson's blinks eventually synchronized with the falling of every drop. Four hours passed in that silence. As the fifth hour neared, the phone rang. It echoed and Gibson jumped.

Jansen said into her two-way, "Gibson is in play. Is everything set?"

"We're good on this end," Tess said. "Tracking is on, and we're recording."

"How long will Gibson have to stay on for?"

"Not long, maybe fifteen seconds."

"Okay then. Cell phones off, everyone. You have to stay on the line for at least fifteen seconds, Vernon, so make this believable."

Everyone clipped on an earpiece.

Nodding and clearing his throat, Gibson extended a shaking hand and grabbed the receiver. His dry voice rasped a "Hello."

The agents listened through the earpieces. Dormer looked at his watch.

"Vernon Gibson?"

The same chilly voice that Gibson described in his initial interrogation was that of Dr. Moira Grey. It was she who was on the line now, tightening the noose around Josh Anderson's neck.

"Who is this?"

"Don't be stupid. November eighth, nine-forty a.m.. The two trucks will be crossing the bridge, on the lower level. Modify your schedules accordingly. Do not use the bridge after eight a.m. — the attack will be at about nine-forty."

Gibson froze, seemingly afraid. The receiver continued to shake in his hand. Dormer nudged him, mouthing "Keep going."

"Why are you doing this?" Gibson asked.

"To help you. We would like to continue using your services into the future. The attack may affect your business and that wouldn't help *our* business if we need you in the future."

Jansen looked at Dormer who was still looking at his watch. He looked up and shook his head. Jansen rallied Gibson on.

"I-I have a shipment of guns coming in soon from Brazil. If you're interested..."

"You will be contacted when we need you."

"Wait!"

The line went empty.

"Did we get it?" Jansen asked.

"If we did it was just barely," Dormer said.

"Tess?"

"Yeah, we got it. Hold on." After several seconds, "She must've been using a scrambler. The computer's saying the call originated from several places around the country."

The room let out a collective, frustrated sigh.

Dormer walked over and put his hand on Gibson's shoulder. "About that shipment of guns..."

Graham's office was dimly lit as usual. He was at his desk, popped two .50 milligram Tramadol and washed it down with several large swallows from a bottle of Aquafina.

"This is too easy, David," Jansen said, sitting on the other side of the AD's desk. "Why give away such vital information to someone you don't know — especially to someone so high on the NCTC list."

"Gibson operated unchecked in this country for three years, even longer abroad. Since he's run lucrative businesses before — and because he's been pretty lucky here — Anderson probably thought he was a safe bet. Besides, I somehow doubt Josh Anderson has a copy of the NCTC list."

"Anderson's profile doesn't reflect that. He wouldn't make an amateur mistake like this. He's too logical and he's too careful. It's why he's stayed free and alive as long as he has. I'm telling you, Anderson is too smart for this."

"He could find these people through mediators. This may not have been his fault. Bottom line is we either catch him or one of his associates, we sweat 'em, and we get our questions answered."

"That woman on the phone could be lying."

"What do you mean?"

"I donno, like I said, this is too easy. We get lucky on Gibson, he flips in no time, and Anderson — a well-known and highly intelligent dissident — falls into our laps, after making a beginner's mistake. It's reading like a script, David."

"Are you saying that Gibson and this woman are setting us up?"

"They could be working with Anderson and give us a fake target to distract us. Or…"

"Or…?"

"Or they're setting Anderson up."

"Who would *they* be?" Graham asked

"I don't know. I'm just throwing ideas out here."

"We haven't found anything to support that Gibson's lying to us. The polygraph came back…"

"…The polygraph can be beaten."

"Just like in the movies," Graham said acerbically.

Jansen stared back at Graham, unyielding.

"So what do you want to do, Andrea?"

"Sweat him."

"*Sweat him?* There's no way his lawyer will sign off on that. If we do it anyway, Gibson and his lawyer will bring us up on some civil rights bullshit."

"There will only be blowback if we're wrong."

"We can't risk a lawsuit. They'll shut us down."

"But we could risk the lives of thousands, right?"

"You're just speculating,"

"Call it a hunch."

"Same difference."

"Not entirely."

"You have no evidence to support this."

"If we don't do everything to stop this attack from happening then we'll be shutdown and probably lose our jobs; and on top of that, we'll be as responsible as Anderson."

The Tramadol had just kicked in, and now, because of Jansen, the Valium was losing speed. Graham paused, and noticed he was short of breath. He took several deep breaths, refocused, then told Jansen he would call Gibson's lawyer.

"Thank you, David."

"Where are we on the Anderson attack?" Graham quickly digressed.

"Well there's no way Anderson would still go through with the attack if we close the bridge down. If anything he would just move to another bridge, or God knows where else. Besides it'd be commuter hell."

"We should run as if business as usual. Set up undercover agents as repair details for the next couple of days in case the woman was lying. Call the MTA and have all their trains that usually cross the bridge go through the tunnel on the R or W lines until further notice. We'll post units two miles from the bridge so we can see the trucks coming. There will also be units on the bridge posing as commuters, and morning joggers. We'll have them stop in front of the trucks — pretend there's car trouble or something like that— and we'll start the counterattack from there. Do you think that with his back against the wall Anderson will detonate the C-4 anyway?"

"There's nothing in his profile that would suggest he's a fanatic, so on the surface I'd say no. But you don't have to be a fanatic to be okay with the concept of dying."

"We'll need helicopter support for the ground units. I'll call the FBI upstairs and see if they could lend us some extra bodies on top of the Counterterrorist teams."

"Has local been informed?" Jansen asked.

"Yeah. They're sending us SIS and SWAT teams."

"I didn't know we had an interagency protocol in effect."

"It's in place as of this morning. Us along with the NYPD are all sharing the same network until this crisis is over."

"Who has rank?"

"We do, and you'll have ranking on the bridge when you're down there."

"If there are injured?"

"EMS and medivac units will be on standby."

"Where am I going to be stationed?"

"On the ground. Jim was a sniper for the Marines so he'll be in the helicopter covering you guys on the ground. I want you to be in one of the cars set to stop the trucks."

"How much force are you authorizing?"

"Make it quick and clean."

"How should we handle the hostiles?"

"Use your own discretion, but I'm getting squeezed from Up On High about Anderson. Try to take him alive if possible. Vegas wants him alive to be extradited back to them and stand trial, but if Anderson and his rogues gallery become too much of a threat, take them out. As long as it's self-defense or in defense of a civilian no one will lose any sleep over it. If the shit gets thick out there, I don't want you to hesitate. Loss of life other than theirs is unacceptable. Am I clear?"

"Crystal."

Jansen lingered.

"What is it?"

"Why would they only target the lower level of the bridge? Why not split up, one on the higher, one on the lower?"

"If they use the lower level they can cause a maximum in structural damage and casualties — four lines of trains plus commuters driving to work during rush hour. Also, by using the lower level the chances of getting a clean shot from any kind of air strike are reduced. If everything goes well, Jim should be able to pick them off if they're drawn in the open."

"When was he in the Marines?"

"During the Gulf War, but he's been brushing up. He'll be good-to-go by Tuesday morning."

"Good," Jansen said.

"On the day-of I'll be running point with Liz feeding real time info from our satellite hookup to everyone in the field. We're giving you guys as much support out there as possible. We have to be real careful — there are going to be a lot of pedestrians on that bridge, even more so than usual because of the morning rush hour. I don't want any unwarranted loss of life, and no collateral damage."

"I understand, sir. I'll do my best."

"I know you will."

The implications of what Graham had said — the objective — hadn't registered at first. More likely than not Jansen would be facing the possibility of death more so than she ever had in the past, and more likely than not, she would be forced to take a life — something that she had never done, despite her years of field work. The possibility of dying no longer worried her, but as experience taught her and as Besson predicted, there was a slight hesitation considering there was someone of weight in her life.

The rest of the afternoon was a blur to her. Her mind—although it had put off thinking about what to say to Besson—she was unable to stop thinking about murdering someone. When in the field there is just as high a chance that you would have to kill as you are likely to be killed. It's a fact, it's part of the oath, and it's something that never bothered her.

Raised in a strict Christian home, Jansen was raised believing that killing — regardless of the reason or situation — was a sin. Although she no longer identified herself with religion she still believed that killing was never an answer — that there was always a better solution. When she became a field agent she considered her hesitation to kill to be her greatest weakness, and her instructors told her that her hesitation could one day get her killed. She was the best shot in her class, and it made her feel somewhat ashamed. The only thing that would make her feel more shame was the fact that she had never overcome that hesitation, and she hated how she thought — as did others — that her hesitation to kill was a weakness. "It's just the kind of world we live in right now," she would tell herself. Her observation was not inaccurate, and she had no reason to feel ashamed for her apprehension.

At the computer in her office, Jansen brought up Anderson's file. She looked over his record — the bombings. Eighty-five people dead. The stadium assassination of Senator Alan Kessler that caused a riot in which fifty more people lost their lives and another hundred-twenty were injured. Jansen realized then that there was a distinction between killing and murdering and kept telling herself: It's just the kind of world we live in right now.

At the same moment Jansen brought up Anderson's file, Will Besson shuffled into his apartment. His cell phone rang, and knew immediately who was calling when he saw the blue screen flash, CALL FROM: UN-AVAILABLE.

"Besson, it's me," Lavalle said.

"I know. Is everything okay?"

"Fine. I just wanted to tell you that we're going to be shipping soon. We followed your instructions to the letter. You'll receive a pick-up receipt in the mail a few days from now."

"Good."

"You're going to need help with installation."

"I'll make do."

"You'll attract attention. You'll have help."

"From who? Anderson and his group? It's too dangerous."

"We used one of Anderson's men — paid him off to keep his mouth shut. He had connections we needed. But, to answer your question, no: I'm using some of the people I worked with in the past. A sleeper cell of sorts."

"Thanks for letting me know so quickly," Besson replied, shocked and more irritated by Lavalle's cornucopia of secrets, deceptions and half-truths. "Are you sure I can trust these people and that they're not under surveillance?"

"I can vouch for these people, Will. I handpicked them for this task myself, and I double- and triple-checked their information from the Interpol database. They don't have anything on these people."

"When were you going to tell me about all this?"

"Today."

Son of a bitch. "You should've told me about this sooner," he growled. "If even *one thing* goes wrong..."

"It won't," Lavalle replied.

"ETA?" he said, knowing he was beaten.

"November fifth; seven A.M. Port of New York."

With that, Besson resolved that the next act would contain a great deal of change and alarming progression.

17

Dorsia was a high-end restaurant on the lower East Side. Born from the once fictitious restaurant of the same name in Bret Easton Ellis's *American Psycho*, Dorsia was meant to, and with much success, taken from its story bound counterpart the excesses of decorum, food, alcohol and inaccessibility to those who weren't on specific lists or whose names wouldn't do much for their rating in Zagat.

Those who were in on the joke found Dorsia to be an amusing example of the influence of pop culture on the upper crust of society. Those who weren't were consigned to the aggravation that comes from having yet another high-end restaurant where reservations were impossible to make if you didn't have the right name.

Upon his return to New York, Martin Strughold was reminded by his secretary of reservations he had made months earlier, and remembering how adamant Besson was on having a sit-down, decided to commit to both duties at once. Letting Besson know ahead of time, Strughold told him to dress up — referring to the dress code as borderline presidential.

Strughold was taking his time with the wine list, settling on a Chard just as Besson was being escorted to the table by the maître d'. He was dressed in a suit — black over a dark blue dress shirt with a red striped tie. Strughold was impressed.

He gave a strong handshake and a kind smile. "You clean up good."

"Surprised?"

"Considering your daily attire consists of a leather jacket and jeans I'd have to say yeah. When was the last time you wore as suit, anyway? Watergate?"

Besson laughed. "I must've aged well if you think I'm that old."

"Will, if you're this worried about your age now just imagine how bad you'll feel when you get to mine."

They both laughed. Then Besson said, "I figured I should listen to your demands — dressing up and all — I really wasn't in the mood to have to listen to you if I embarrass you in front of your upper-crust friends."

Strughold laughed boisterously. "You flatter me. I had to make the reservations here months ago, and I had to pay another hundred to the maître d' to add another seat to the table at the last minute."

The off-white coloring of Dorsia was elegant, the lighting was dimmed but not low. Candles hung from the walls. Everyone was well dressed. Besson thought he spotted the Mayor.

"I doubt they serve chili dogs."

"They serve it under an expensive cream sauce or amouse bouche." Strughold laughed to himself. "Don't worry — I took the liberty of ordering for both of us."

"Tell me what you ordered for me and we'll see how I feel."

"You're better off not knowing."

"I probably wouldn't recognize it anyway."

"And it costs more than the pension deal you got from the Bureau."

"Ha."

The waiter, his practiced smile pasted on, served the Chardonnay and asked if the gentlemen would like to hear the specials of the evening. Besson said "Sure," certain he'd get a personal kick out of it. But Strughold kyboshed it.

Besson noticed Strughold moving the wine around in his glass in is hand to let it breathe before taking a nose-deep smell. "What whiskey do you have?" he asked.

"We have Jameson, John Walker blue and black..."

"How much for a dram of sixty year old Macallan?"

Strughold nearly choked on his Chard. "Just get him a double Jack on the rocks."

"Very good," replied the waiter.

Once the waiter was out of earshot Strughold looked toward an amused Besson. "You're a fucking asshole."

Heads half-turned and people recognized him. Strughold didn't care.

Besson laughed. "Just seeing how fancy their bar is. How was your trip?"

"The flight was the only saving grace. You'd think once you've been away from your stomping ground long enough you'd learn to miss it in some way. As a home, DC has lost its charm.

"But then I suppose you could say that about any city: once the surroundings have become familiar — too familiar — when you know the very pulse of it, its likes and dislikes, its heart and soul… once you truly know a city, it begins to lose the charm of its mystery, because you've already mastered and decoded it."

"Subtext would say you were talking about your wife."

Strughold laughed. "Hardly." Another laugh. "I don't even remember what she looks like."

"So what was that? Did you crib from Horace or Whitman or what?"

Strughold winked and took a sip of his wine. "Actually I think it was a Besson."

Besson faked a smile and downed the Chard.

"You should've savored it. You don't want to know how much that glass cost me."

Besson winked, knowing that his act would set Strughold off. "Life's too short."

The waiter returned with their dinner and Besson's drink.

"Ahh, faithful boy with my medicine."

"Am I to suspect that you're angry with the decisions Peter made?" Strughold inquired.

"What makes you say that?"

"The fact you haven't mentioned him yet."

Besson rolled his eyes. "Well, yeah, I'm damned angry. I don't like being kept in the dark. This is a three-way street, Martin."

"It'll all work out, Will. I'm telling you. His man thinks they're moving the C-4. Anderson's men are pissants like you said. They're scared of men like us. Scared of men in suits with actual authority."

"Just keep me in the damn loop."

Strughold nodded.

The main course was served.

The dinner was unrecognizable as Strughold had warned. Tasted like beef. Halfway through Strughold said, "From what I've heard from Peter, your relationship with Anderson hasn't much improved."

"I trust only what I know."

"Ahh, the consummate skeptic-detective, relying on his hard science, rejecting the inconsistent and immeasurable attributes of instinct."

"No, I do actually listen to my instincts, and they tell me not to trust them fully."

Strughold laughed. "Is that why you asked to see me?"

"No."

"I'm not a DT like you; spell it out for me, then."

Besson took a healthy mouthful of his drink. "I'm seeing someone."

Strughold shrugged. "Mazel Tov."

"She's the woman I mentioned to you. Andrea."

"The one from DC? What is she doing here?"

"Transfer to New York."

"She's still with the Bureau, then."

"Yeah."

Strughold, eyes widened, downed his Chard. In a different situation, Besson would've laughed. Even now, he fought a smile.

Besson said, "Listen, before you..."

"Too late. She's working for the Bureau, yes?"

"Yeah."

Strughold hissed, "She's working for the Bureau and you're conspiring to blow up a fucking city. This is in-fucking-sane."

"She could be an early warning system," Besson reasoned, though knowing he wasn't going to use her that way. "Let us know if anything's up."

"Do you think she'll give you a call fifteen minutes before HRT knocks on your door and double taps you in the head?"

"Having her as a resource is further insurance so that wouldn't happen."

"Risk versus reward, my dear Will." Strughold paused, reading him. "Is that the only reason you're with her?"

Silent.

"Oh, fuck me." He paused a beat. "Oh, wait, yeah, you are right now." The silence made the air heavy. Strughold was damned angry. "So when you go on the lam, do you think she'll go with you? Some Beauty and the Beast, Starling-Lecter thing? Be real."

Besson glared at him, deferred his anger. He had a right. "She wouldn't have to know."

"That's a helluva secret," Strughold scoffed. "And you two leaving the country or wherever the hell you're going right before the bomb goes off is just some massive coincidence." A dark thought. "Does she know you work for me?"

"She knows I work for Halifax. I told her I was a consultant," Besson replied. "And a lot of people travel on holidays."

Strughold laughed and winked. "Amazing job *consulting* so far I might add. But how many consultants have a Swiss bank account?"

"She shouldn't have to die."

"What makes *her* different?"

"I-she…"

Strughold nodded, understanding. "Ahh, I see. But let me ask you something: when this disaster hits and you want to go off and live a quiet life, and she wants to go back to Washington and keep fighting the good fight, what then?"

"She'll be alive at least."

Strughold paused. "If you were so hung up on this and so sure of what you were going to do, why come to me with this?"

"You're involved in this as much as I am and I know what kind of breach in security this could be. You deserved to know."

Strughold seemed appeased. "You're a good man, Will. If she's what floats your boat, I say God bless. But remember to think with the right head."

———————

———————

18

November

Every day shipments of cargo are imported to American harbors. The numbers of shipments and cargo range in the millions. Less than two percent of those are ever searched by authorities for illicit materials. If someone wanted to smuggle in any illegal materials, the likelihood of it getting noticed would be slim, especially if superfluous precautions were taken. It was that route of transit that Besson suggested to smuggle in the hydrogen bomb.

The bomb was placed in a crate that bore the emblem of a winery that was no longer in business, and the crate was loaded onto a cargo ship destined for New York, scheduled to arrive on November fifth — the day of Besson's thirty-ninth birthday. The irony continued to peck at him as he waited at the Port of New York.

Two days earlier Besson had received a letter with a remailing stamp on it which gave the impression that it came from Las Vegas, and the stamp under that suggested it came from outside the country. Inside was the pick-up receipt that Besson needed along with an ID for a man he didn't recognize. The name on the ID matched the name on the pick-up slip. Besson was wary of relying on the sleepers, trusting only his own work. He pocketed both and tore up the envelope.

The sky was gray, and the ground was wet from the storm the night before. A cloud of mist was hanging over the Manhattan Bridge. A cold front had moved in just recently, and Besson stood leaning against the brick wall of the shipyard's main office, wearing his aviator sunglasses to conceal his face. He was feeling great apprehension because the sleepers that Lavalle had inserted in New York — the ones that were supposed to meet him here — were fifteen minutes late. It wasn't the lateness that necessarily bothered him, it was the belief that they were present and observing him from afar. Lavalle's near-paranoia irritated Besson like a hot needle at the back of his neck.

Finally, a dark mass slowly formed deep within the fog and began to separate from the morning mist. After another eight minutes, as the cargo ship was making final preparations for docking, a black panel truck quickly drove up, and a man and a woman stepped out.

Lavalle the Predictable.

He continued to watch the cargo ship, glancing at the panel truck out of the corner of his eye. He knew who they were.

Three others filed out of the truck.

That's right, look suspicious, look like goddamn amateurs.

The man and the woman who stepped out of the van waved the others off, and they reentered the panel truck.

Better.

The two walked over to Besson and greeted him. Besson kept looking at the cargo ship. They seemed to be taken aback, as Besson wanted. He had to let them know whose mission it was in the first place. They took their orders from him, always. He merely nodded to their greeting; his gaze remained attentively on the cargo ship. At his leisure — a count to twenty — he turned and looked at them.

The man was taller than Besson, older as well. His somewhat long black hair was peppered with white strands. His face was worn, and his eyes reflected a weariness Besson didn't care for. Besson realized his was the picture on the ID he received in the mail. A forced partnership.

Lavalle the Manipulator.

The woman was smaller, with curly brown hair, and too young to be doing this kind of work. She was presumptuous enough to firmly believe it was she who was in control.

"Besson," the woman greeted again. "I'm Martha Dench."

The long haired man introduced himself in a gravelly, almost bored voice. "Marcus Gardner."

Besson slid the ID out of his pocket.

"Your ID says Mitchell White. Lavalle's being careful, right?"

"Right." Besson passed the ID to him. Then the man asked, "Do you have the shipping receipt?"

"Yes." But Besson didn't offer it.

The dock was also a loading point for cargo. It was set to be loaded onto the backs of eighteen-wheelers (housed in the next warehouse) and driven to the designated locations. However, Besson would be picking up his own cargo, to ensure that the crate in which it had traveled hadn't been tampered with, and to ensure that there would be no traceable location where could be discovered. A personal pick-up of this kind was highly irregular and fairly suspicious. Besson knew it and was unnerved.

There was an uncomfortable silence hanging over them for fifteen minutes, waiting for the ship to reach port.

Frank Crowley, a small, overweight and bearded man dressed in a dirty baseball cap and stained white t-shirt over a beaten North Face coat, walked toward the three silent individuals.

"You were the ones that called about the pickup," Crowley said as he took several heaving breaths through his mouth. "We got it; I just need to see a pickup receipt and an ID."

Besson handed him the receipt and Gardner handed him the ID. Crowley looked at them with a slight confusion, which bordered on suspicion, Besson thought.

"The computer said a Mitch Warren or something was the name on the receipt. Which one of you is him?"

"That would be me," Gardner said. "Mitchell White. It's all there."

Crowley was staring at Dench. Gardner moved closer to her and Besson cleared his throat loudly.

"We don't get a lotta people that pick their things up directly. We use these ships for big imports. You sure this is what you want?" Crowley asked.

"Yes," Dench said, rather emphatically.

Crowley's mouth veered into a crooked smile that vanished quickly as he looked down at the ID and the receipt.

"We're friends of Anderson," Besson said softly.

"You cops?"

"No."

Crowley smirked. "Everything seems fine here. I'll punch your order number into the computer." Looking at Dench he said, "Where do ya want it?"

"In the panel truck would be fine," Gardner cut in.

Crowley looked at Gardner and repeated, "I'll just go find out what crate your thing is in and my boys'll bring it on over."

Besson watched as Crowley walked away and felt a familiar uneasiness from him, but tried to ignore it. Gardner watched Crowley at the computer to make sure he didn't suspect anything.

"Find out where this guy lives," Besson ordered. "and tap his phone conversations from now on. At home and here."

"Do you think he suspects something?" Dench asked.

"In case he does I want to be notified."

"Are you always this worried?"

"It's better safe…" Besson stopped himself, comprehending very suddenly whose inflections he was borrowing. He cleared his throat. "It's better to be safe than sorry." A beat. "Is everything in place for the installation?"

"Not yet."

"Why?"

"That's my fault," Gardner said. "the job I took on is going to require me a little more time until I can move around more freely."

"How much time?" Besson's voice was irked.

"I've been working there for about three months now. They trust me a lot; all I need is another few weeks."

"What kind of job is it?"

"Exactly as Mr. Lavalle said you'd need."

"Are you sure we're going to stay on schedule?"

"I'll be able to get us spare clothes, secure a van, and have official papers to go with it," Gardner replied.

"Good."

"We're good at what we do," Dench said to Besson, prideful.

Crowley returned and told them that everything checked out and their shipment was being unloaded as they spoke. He seemed intimidated.

A forklift was used to bring the rather large crate to the van, and the men in the van pulled it in from inside. They inspected the crate, found no damage to the structure and no signs of tampering. Besson checked all the same.

Gardner handed an envelope to Crowley.

"This should cover the fee... and yours."

Before Crowley even processed it, the transaction had ended. Besson left in his car, followed by the panel truck.

"No one's ever picked their shit up directly," a worker said to Crowley.

"Yeah."

"More people like that, we'd lose our jobs."

"Yeah."

Once off the main strip leading from the docks, both vehicles stopped. The side of the panel truck open, Martha Dench stared at Besson.

"Do you have a place for this thing?" Besson asked.

"Yeah. We rented a warehouse."

"Run a diagnostic on the bomb. Make sure it wasn't tampered with. Contact me when things are ready on your end."

"Sure."

Besson then sped off, heading back towards civilization, driving on streets wet from a recent storm. The sound of the tires skidding through the water reassured him; it was the only sound to be heard for miles.

19

Tom Sabian was a public defender commonly used by the NYPD for those who couldn't afford their own attorney. After twelve years as a public defender he opened up his own practice in 1997, hoping to make more money. Following a lawsuit against him (still pending), Sabian returned to the public defender's office while keeping his private cases so he could make enough extra money to hire a lawyer after the judge declined his request to represent himself.

Though only forty-five, in the past year he seemed to have aged another twenty and more of his hair had fallen out. His eyes were tired and it seemed as if the fight had been taken out of him.

Elizabeth Tess observed this about Sabian, as well as the heaving stomach pushing through the shirt of his suit. He didn't notice that his slacks were too short.

Sabian followed Tess down the dull blue-gray hallway down to the interrogation room where Gibson was waiting for him. He was appointed Gibson's attorney after the Justice Department froze all of his funds and Gibson found himself broke.

Gibson was asleep on the table in the interrogation room when Sabian was escorted in.

"They'll be with you in a moment," Tess said.

Sabian nudged Gibson, who groaned.

Graham and Jansen watched from the other side of the one-way mirror.

"Vernon," Sabian said. "What's wrong? You look like shit."

"I haven't been sleeping. They've been keeping me up."

"Asking you questions?"

"I guess."

"Like what?"

"I donno. Stuff."

"Let me see your eyes."

"Why?"

"Did you use anything? Any drugs or something like that?"

"No!"

"Well you're sweating, and you're talking slow, and you're pale. Let me see your eyes."

"I didn't do anything. I'm telling you, they've been keeping me up."

"Should we be listening in on them?" Jansen asked Graham; they were watching from the other side of the One-way.

"I won't tell if you won't."

"Do you know anything about Gibson's lawyer?"

"Sabian? Yeah. Liz gave me his file. He's a rent-a-lawyer with a pending lawsuit against him. He crawled up from the sewer with Gibson."

Jansen looked for something recognizable in Graham's face, but found nothing. Instead there was something burning, something shameful; something that was brought to light unwittingly by Gibson. It was something that wounded him, Jansen was sure of it.

"Jesus Christ, they're bloodshot," Sabian said.

"He's not stoned," Jansen said to Graham. "He's sleep deprived and scared, but not stoned."

"I've had him under twenty-four-hour watch. I told Dobson to make a loud noise every fifteen minutes, and I raised the heat in the room here eight degrees when they brought him in," Graham confessed, his voice full of personal satisfaction.

"Good one," Jansen muttered dryly.

"Okay, look, just sit tight." Sabian reached for a candy bar in his pocket. "Eat this, keep your sugar up. When they come in just let me do all the talking and you'll be okay."

"That's our cue," Graham said in an excited tone that reminded Jansen of something terrible.

Introductions were skipped by Sabian who began as soon as Graham and Jansen entered the room.

"What have you done to my client?" Sabian said, outraged. "He's malnourished and sleep deprived and I'm told that you now want to pump him full of drugs."

"I'm sure it's not a foreign concept for your client."

"You can't talk about my client—"

"*Your client* has admitted to doing business with known terrorists. *Your client* is an accomplice and *your client* is a known smuggler."

"He's also still an American citizen with rights! You already have the results of the polygraph—"

"The polygraph can be manipulated."

"And it's also inadmissible in court," Sabian said, as if he discovered a snake in his garden. "Is that why you want to drug my client? I will not allow my client to continue under these conditions."

Sabian continued on his seemingly rehearsed Rights of Prisoners rant, with Graham yelling back at him, hot tempered.

Jansen started pouring over a copy of Gibson's papers that gave him immunity from being prosecuted for treason when her eyes brightened.

In a calm but firm tone, Jansen read aloud, "'…Document becomes binding once all necessary investigative measures are administered and exhausted, proving beyond all reasonable doubt that the person/persons in question are telling the truth.' If Mr. Gibson decides not to take the sodium pentothal, his immunity will be expunged."

"If convicted he could serve another twenty years minimum, not including the other charges," Graham said, recovering his normal tone. "He could face a maximum of life imprisonment for treason — that is, if he escapes the needle of course."

Sabian felt his case and his redemption slipping, as well as the sweat on the nape of his neck growing cold.

"So whaddya wanna do, my boy?" Graham said to Gibson.

Gibson looked at Sabian who was distant. Gibson was screwed, and he knew it.

Suddenly Tess burst into the room, "Andrea, David, I need to talk to you two outside for a second."

"What is it?" Graham said, once they separated from Sabian and Gibson.

"You guys can't give Gibson the serum — he's allergic to it."

"Why didn't you tell us this before?"

"We only had a partial medical history. We just got the rest in now."

"How bad is the allergy?" Jansen asked.

"Fatal."

"We won't be able to make this fly. Goddamnit."

"Then what do we do?" Tess asked.

Graham looked through the one-way then back to Tess and Jansen.

"Let him go and do the best we can at the trial and on Tuesday. Cut 'em loose, Liz. I'm sorry, Andrea. We'll just have to wait."

Three days left.

20

After work Jansen quickly made her way to D'Agostino's to pick up a birthday cake which she'd had personalized, then headed to the liquor store for a bottle of cheap champagne. Taste deferred to the sought after-effect. At every birthday after thirty, the champagne became cheaper and stronger. One in the eye of time.

When she initially brought it up, Besson insisted that she buy him nothing, but eventually he met her halfway, as long as it was something small. She purposely forgot to listen to their agreement.

It took half a dozen phone calls and a creative redefining of Proper Use of Authority, but she finally obtained Besson's gift; specially packaged by a friend at the Smithsonian, and shipped it first-class.

Once at home Jansen showered immediately, hoping to wash off the sleazy memory of Tom Sabian. It was a horrid, slippery feeling. Thinking about it reminded her of Gibson and the small detail that may have kept the FBI from knowing more about the case, a case that had been a source of confusion since it began, a source of great turmoil and possible deception. That small detail in Gibson's medical records that could greatly impede their investigation. The investigation. The bridge. Tuesday. Anderson. Getting frustrated again. Damn it all.

As the steam filled up the bathroom, Jansen watched her reflection in the mirror fade. She stepped in, and the hot water began to heal. The water from the shower head dripped down rhythmically, pattering on the ceramic bottom. Her muscles relaxed and the aching in her bones subsided, and the world that was her job drifted away in clouds of steam.

After her shower she dressed in a navy blue blouse, a black skirt with gray pinstripes and high heels, and a pink ribbon in her down flowing hair. She almost never wore a skirt or high heels, but it was a special occasion after all. Jansen had very shapely legs.

Besson had just returned from Dean & Deluca with a precooked meal when Jansen arrived.

"Happy Birthday!" Jansen said, handing Besson the birthday cake.

"Thank you," Besson replied, sheepishly. "You look great."

"You don't look so bad yourself."

They kissed, and Jansen handed over the gift.

"I hope you like Dean and DeLuca," he said.

"Sounds great."

They ate their precooked dinners at the table in Besson's kitchen, passing each other half-smiles. They'd checked their other lives at the door.

Besson laughed. "Yeah."

"You seem quiet," Jansen said after a while.

Besson chewed for several seconds and nodded. "I'm a little... elsewhere."

"What's wrong?"

"Nothing." *Liar.*

"Liar."

Besson smiled to himself, and was both surprised and fairly panicked at Jansen's incredible ability to see through him.

"So what's wrong?"

"It's nothing... just my birthday I guess."

"Imagine what'll happen when you turn forty," Jansen mused, "but the sports car would sweeten the deal."

"Yes indeed, but I think fifty will be the big mark."

"What do you see for yourself then?"

"Zoloft, hair dye and a noose."

Besson and Jansen laughed heartily. The champagne bottle was emptied within twenty minutes.

Next was the birthday cake; Jansen placed a candle in the middle and lit it from a match.

"Make a wish," she said with a smile.

After dinner, Jansen, who stumbled in her high heels — due partly to her inexperience in them and partly because of the champagne — picked up the small festive gift bag from the couch and handed it to Besson. He tripped on the living room table, but pretended it didn't happen.

"Smooth move."

"I used to be a dancer."

"Happy Birthday."

Besson slipped the gift out of the bag, revealing Edgar Allen Poe's *The Purloined Letter*, in parchment and handwritten, bound and secured in a portfolio. It could very well be the original. It was. The alcohol allowed him to excuse the dark irony, and he smiled affectionately despite it. A truly remarkable gift.

"Do you like it?"

"Of course," he replied, bemused. He eventually collected himself and rediscovered his dry note. "but what happened to 'keeping it small'?"

"Must've forgotten," she said wryly

"You're a sly one. How did you get this?"

"A friend at the Smithsonian and a few people who got nervous hearing from a federal agent. Besides, I know how much you like detective stories, so I got you an original copy of the first detective story ever written."

"Doesn't that fall under the Abuse of Power radar?"

"I won't tell if you won't."

"You're secret is definitely on the Q.T."

"I guess you really do like it then."

"You… know me too well."

Besson looked into her incandescent blue eyes and drew her by her face in for a tender kiss.

Besson, even at this stage, had no idea why he decided to include her in it. He never pumped her for information, and he constantly had second thoughts about his decisions. However, whatever sense of foreboding and misgivings he had dissipated once he was in her presence. When with her, Besson felt he was able to live a life with her that he could've seen to its end, in a different time or a different world. Now, though, it was a non-issue.

There was a mission to complete. For now, all he wanted to do was escape into an unattainable dream.

The secrets they kept allowed them to live in a world separate from their fretful realities, and in this world they were entirely different people. Together they were two regular people, in a simpler world full of warm gazes, and lovers' stares. They created a world in the other, outside of the screeching sounds of the city, beyond the constraints of honor and duty. Their world can be found in either one of their apartments, in any restaurant they frequent and any place they met. A world of sweet rapture, reality had no jurisdiction there.

That had been the basis or their relationship from its birth, the quiet relationship that dared not speak its name in public. He was her instructor, back then, the one who told her that her hesitation to use her service weapon could get her killed. It was a working relationship that evolved quickly despite their six-year age difference and despite what it would've meant for their careers if the nature of their relationship had been disclosed at the time. They made love for the first time the night before her graduation at a hotel far from her quarters and his apartment. Afterwards, as they listened to the radio, she had asked him what his favorite song was. In his driest wit, he told her it was classified.

Secrets allow us to live more leisurely, sometimes more exciting, lives. The illusion is comforting, so long as the real world doesn't seep in through the cracks that come with its conception. The hull of desire can only take so much pressure. All it takes is one small breach for the entire structure to sink.

21

Tuesday, November 8th

Andrea Jansen was up at five. She dressed in cargo pants — extra magazines can be stored easily in its deep pockets — sneakers, a sweater and a long coat to cover her Glock.

In the mirror, she caught a glimpse of herself with the Glock in the shoulder holster. She remembered her days of Catechism, reciting the Rosary, the promises she made under the eyes of God as she was confirmed into church. She wore a cross around her neck, given to her by her grandmother on the day of her confirmation. She had never taken it off.

Faith is something you have as a child, and it's something that gets picked apart piece by piece by the depredation of reality, the way a vulture gnaws a cadaver. It's something that you eventually grow out of in favor of reality.

The badge at her hip tugged heavily. *The oaths we take*, Jansen thought. She steadied herself, checked the time, and headed for the door.

When she arrived the FBI office was already crowded and loud, filled with SIS and SWAT teams, the team the FBI gave out on loan, undercover agents dressed as city workers, and the usual Bureau staff.

Jansen spotted Graham at the other end of the office as she passed through the electronic doors. Graham saw her and waved her over. Next to him was Jim Dormer, an older man dressed in a suit, about fifty, and Assistant Director Bill Hamlin.

Jansen and Hamlin nodded to each other respectfully. Jansen never forgot it was Bill Hamlin who had accepted her transfer when every other agency had branded her as a troublemaker. She noticed hints of gray in his hair, coming in at the root.

"Welles Cochrane, this is Special Agent in Charge Andrea Jansen. She'll also be running the show in the field this morning."

"Pleasure to meet you," Cochrane said.

"Mr. Cochrane is the SAC of the Vegas office," Graham explained. "He's come here on good will to oversee this situation."

"We can handle ourselves just fine," she said.

Hamlin stirred, anxiously.

"Not really *oversee*," Cochrane replied. "I'm merely observing. I'm really here to see that Josh Anderson and his compatriots are brought back for trial."

"Considering Anderson and his compatriots are only based in Nevada, but planning and overseeing an attack here in New York, don't you think we should also have a say where he's extradited; or at least where he's put on trial."

"Andrea," Hamlin warned, "Agent Cochrane is only here to help."

"We'd better get started," Graham suggested quickly.

"Ball breaker," Dormer whispered to Jansen with a smirk.

"Can I have everybody's attention please?" Graham began. "In a few minutes, we're going to be underway. As you all already know the Manhattan Bridge is set to be attacked by two dump trucks of C-4. The man heading up this assault — Josh Anderson — is expected to be there on the bridge today. While the primary objective is to stop the C-4 from detonating, our friends in Las Vegas would prefer that Josh Anderson is captured alive, but if the shit hits the fan deadly force is authorized."

Cochrane shot Graham a look. Jansen noticed, and shot him one in return.

"Right now, I would like to hand the floor over to Andrea Jansen, the agent in charge of the counterattack."

"Good morning," Jansen said. "We're running behind, so I'll be brief. The attack is supposed to begin at nine-forty. Every team is to be deployed and ready by seven sharp and teams are to be in full body armor. Undercover teams are to wear Kevlar vests under their street clothes.

"This is the layout: SWAT and SIS are going to be on lookout for the dump trucks — license plate numbers and vehicle descriptions are being passed around now. Since traffic is only going Manhattan-bound at this time of day, I want you all deployed on the Brooklyn side from two miles out. I want to see these guys coming.

"Once the dump trucks are in sight, *do not* — I repeat, *do not* — engage them. The BQE will be packed, and we don't need to add to the likelihood of incurring civilian casualties. Alert the rest of us over the COM and prepare to take them at the neck, before they turn onto the bridge. We need to make sure that there aren't any lookouts on their end or any divergent vehicles there to aid them or to grab our attention.

"Undercover units, we've positioned you just short of the center of the bridge. You are to take your positions and disable the trucks if given the word. Jim Dormer and FBI sniper Mike Hurst will be giving us air support which will come in handy if things turn nasty, and David Graham will be running point from here, giving us real time updates from the satellites flying over the area. We should have ample coverage.

"Traffic is relatively light today, which means they'll be moving with at least decent mobility, which means that the danger of incurring civilian deaths is both greater and lesser than before, which means less people on the bridge, but more mobility for Anderson and his team. We do not have the option of a retake, so let's not give Waco an addendum."

The TECH room was dark, the only source of light coming from the many computer screens. With Cochrane in tow, Graham and Tess took their places and fitted themselves with earpieces. They were looking at four screens — satellite shots over the outlying areas from the BQE to the end of the bridge, a digital grid of the units deployed and tracked by GPS systems, real-time coverage of the traffic moving across the bridge, and a tracking screen especially for the helicopter crew.

"Team leaders call in."

"SIS — Fredericks. In position."

"SWAT — Rico. In position."

"FBI — Dalton. In position."

"FBI — Dormer. Ready and raring."

"FBI — Hurst. In position."

"FBI — Jansen. In position."

"Undercover unit — Mainer. In position."

"They're all yours, Andrea," Graham said.

"We are in play. I repeat — all teams are in play. I want total radio silence until the dump trucks are spotted," she said.

There was total silence for well over an hour, when Graham told the helicopter to move further out of the perimeter to avoid suspicion. Every fifteen minutes Jansen demanded updates. There was nothing.

Finally, at a quarter to nine, two dump trucks made their way into visual range of the SWAT team. They called it in.

"They're about fifteen minutes out from the bridge."

"License plates match?" Jansen asked.

"Roger."

"Let them pass, we'll take 'em at the entrance. All teams — we have confirmation."

"Bring 'er around, Jim. It's show-time," Graham said.

"Copy that."

Jansen was riding in an FBI field SUV, and there was another on patrol. One patrol vehicle was to stay ahead of the trucks, the other — Jansen's — was to stay behind. Over the COM came the sound of tires screeching loudly, and for one split second, everyone held their breaths.

Jansen and Graham both yelled into the COM at the same time, demanding an explanation.

"We were just cut off by two sedans," Brenner explained. "We're fine now."

"For Christ's sake, be more careful," Graham barked.

Jansen looked at the onboard computer in the SUV. "I have the targets on the grid. Go around from behind," she told the driver.

"The trucks will reach the entrance in approximately five minutes," Rico reported.

"What was that back there?" Anderson growled into his cell phone.

"Cut off this SUV that was moving too slow," Fredericks replied. "We're still okay, and en route."

"Just be careful."

"Yeah,"

Jansen's SUV was tailing the trucks, several cars behind. "All mobile units: form a floating box around the hostiles."

Anderson looked out his driver's side mirror, and half-noticed the SUV. He looked back again, and felt a the nape of his neck begin to turn red. He could hear Lavalle's voice chiming "better to be safe than sorry." Into his cell he said, "Describe the SUV."

"What? Why?"

"Just do it."

"It was black, pretty big."

Anderson looked into his mirror again.

"Were the windows tinted?"

"I guess so."

"Yes or no. Were they tinted?" his voice was raised.

"Then yes."

"Did you notice any state or federal emblem on the license plate?"

"No."

Although the weather hadn't gotten any warmer, Anderson was beginning to sweat. He pulled the M-6 closer to him.

Lavalle's credo teased his thoughts. *Better safe than sorry.*

"Josh?" Stenger called.

"Alex, when I give the word—floor it."

"What?" Stromm replied.

"Just do it."

"Archer, Mallory, are you in position?"

"We will be shortly," Mallory replied.

"Good. On my word, then."

The SUV was still far enough behind. The trucks began to slow down; the cars behind them began to honk.

"What the fuck? Jansen, do you see this?" Dalton asked.

"Yeah, they're slowing down…"

"You think they're wise?"

"I don't know. David, are you reading in the area?"

"Negative. Jim?"

"Nothing."

Jansen's eyes narrowed.

"Alex?" Anderson called.

"I'm ready."

"Hit it."

The trucks floored, passing in and out of lanes awkwardly with no fore-warning, brakes squealed and tires peeling, short of crashing, as the dump trucks sped quickly towards the bridge.

"Goddamnit, we've been made," Jansen yelled. "SWAT and SIS close in on the bridge. Undercover Unit, the dump trucks just floored it, and they're heading your way full speed. Hit 'em hard."

"Jim, it's Graham. Anderson's wise. Set for rapid-fire shots, multiple targets. Shoot to kill."

Cochrane seized Graham, and turned him around, almost losing his balance when his cane slipped. "What the hell do you think you're do-ing?"

Graham dropped his earpiece, "I'm preventing the wrongful deaths of thousands of people."

"If we do not seize Anderson alive we could very well lose the chance to get the names and locations of God-only-knows how many arms dealers and terrorist cells. It could set entire organizations back *years*."

"And if *I* stop now, the chances of this operation being successful goes down faster than the Queen Mum."

"I have my orders."

"And I have mine," replied Graham, calling for security."

Two uniformed officers enter the TECH room.

"Take Mr. Cochrane someplace to cool off."

"You're making a mistake."

"Get out."

Cochrane was taken out to the main floor, where he shook off the two security guards. He spotted Don Walker and marched over to him.

"Can I help you?"

"I hope so," Cochrane said. "Can you bring up the satellite link?"

"It's not really my field. Can't you go into the TECH room?"

"I really don't want to bother Agent Graham. Why don't you duplicate the patch number from one of the computers?"

"Okay, I'll try."

The feed was routed to Walker's computer, and they watched the screen intently. After several seconds, Cochrane throat went dry.

"Bring up the grid, and put it over the feed."

Walker obliged after several seconds.

"Enhance the grid. Section 9-A." A beat. "My God!"

"What? What is it?"

"Those two sedans in that section. They're in a strategic pattern that vehicles go into to avoid sniper fire."

"Do you think it's—"

"It's deliberate." Cochrane ran back into the TECH room, pushing passed the guards. "Graham, Anderson has a lookout squad."

The two guards reached for Cochrane, but he pulled away from them.

"What's he talking about?" Tess asked.

"The two red sedans. Grid 9-A—"

"Get him out of here!" Graham ordered.

"Damnit Graham, you fucking pillock!"

Cochrane was thrown out again.

"Stay by the door," Graham ordered of the guards.

Cochrane ran back out to the main floor where he grabbed the back of Walker's chair and spun it around to face him.

"The frequency the COM is on. What is it?"

"I don't think I should,"

"If you don't, a lot of people are going to be killed. Those sedans are what, twenty meters from your undercover team. Why? They have no reason to be there. They're waiting for Anderson."

Walker sighed. He patched the frequency number into an earpiece. "You're on."

"Undercover Unit: there are hostiles down further on the service road. They're waiting for—"

"Who is this?" Graham bellowed. "Get off this line now!"

"These hostiles are working in conjunction with Josh Anderson. Take the necessary precautions..."

The two guards came running around the corner from the TECH room to apprehend Cochrane, and under Graham's orders sent him to the interrogation room.

The undercover unit stopped working, and started to their vehicles, looking for their heavier weapons. Mainer and another officer walked toward Cartwright and Stenger. Cartwright discerned what was happening.

The dump trucks were twelve seconds from the Undercover Unit.

Cartwright gained the two officers' attention by walking toward them, then Stenger blasted them both with a silenced handgun. They retrieved the M-6's from the back seats of their cars, and opened fire on the undercover unit, who'd already had them targeted. Cartwright and Stenger took refuge behind their cars and returned fire; the unit was separated between Stenger and Cartwright, while the others waited on the dump trucks.

Traffic heading from the BQE had been dispersed on the neck, because of several near accidents caused by Anderson and Stromm. Jansen and Hammond were left behind, where the traffic was still thick. They made progress going through the service road. Only a few more minutes were left. There was little traffic on the bridge. Jansen was not in any way relieved.

Agents Brenner and Ventrix cut the traffic in half, stopping the SUV diagonally across the two lanes. Traffic redirected itself around. Drivers were speeding. Anderson shot through the windshield of the dump truck, firing at Brenner and Ventrix. When he failed to get a good enough shot, he slouched in his seat as they returned fire, and blasted through the wall made by the SUV. Ventrix was caught in between the two vehicles when they collided, and a torrent of blood spewed from his mouth and decorated the bits of windshield left on the dump truck.

Stromm rammed into the undercover unit, killing two and destroying two other vehicles.

Cartwright and Stenger started to gain an advantage. Stromm climbed to the top of the dump truck and began to rain fire down on the exposed undercover unit.

SIS and SWAT had blocked off any incoming traffic, diverting it to the upper level of the bridge. Jansen and Hammond sped into the area, with Jansen hanging out of door of the SUV, standing on the board-step. With no time to think, she let loose a volley from her Glock. Stromm fell.

Anderson, his head several sizes too big, with a string of blood trickling down his face, grabbed his M-6 slowly. His arms were shaking.

The FBI helicopter dropped down suddenly, flying low, sweeping across the area. Dormer, his finger on the trigger of the M60D yelled, "I have command of the target."

"Take them," Graham ordered.

The bodies of Stenger and Cartwright convulsed as the spray hit them. The helicopter gained altitude and flew into the distance, bringing itself about for another sweep.

Anderson tapped the button of the detonator over and over. No reaction. He was puzzled, and then it suddenly became clear. He had been betrayed by everyone. And he was to take the fall and die.

Anderson wasn't ready to die just yet.

"Secure the area!" Jansen called over the roar of the helicopter.

Anderson waited five beats and popped up into sight, firing in a spray. Jansen hit the ground, hard on her knees and elbows, and heard the sound of a bullet bursting through Hammond's skull. Anderson burst into a run, heading toward the intercrossed steel that acted as a barrier between the trains and the highway. He dropped his M-6, and cut his hips as he attempted squeeze through, onto the tracks.

The bridge began to rumble.

Jansen recovered and was in pursuit.

Anderson ran down the tracks to the gate that separated the tracks from the promenade. He kicked open the gate and continued to run.

Jansen pushed through the barrier easier. The rumbling grew stronger as she hit the tracks. The honking of a train gained her attention, and the headlights burned her eyes. She was on her feet instantly and running towards the gate door. The train did not slow down. She was near the door — she turned and leapt, and felt her ponytail get pushed by the train as it passed.

Jansen readied her gun as joggers hit the ground. Anderson was not too far, limping and clutching his hip.

"Josh Anderson!"

Anderson didn't stop.

One shot to the knee and Anderson fell. He tried to push himself up with one arm, the other hand still at his hip.

"Josh Anderson! Let me see your hands."

Anderson paused and turned suddenly, pointing a handgun, attempting to aim. Jansen was ready first. She double tapped. The gunpowder seared her eyes, but she did not close them — not until Anderson was down on the ground, a pool of blood ever expanding under his mass."

After slowly making her way across the tracks again Jansen stood by the wreckage. It took her a minute to realize she still had the Glock in her hand. She re-holstered it, and glanced at her hands, which weren't shaking. She felt more nauseous. The medivac and EMS teams were already on scene gathering up the wounded members of the undercover unit. SWAT and SIS were stationed all around the bridge on lookout.

Jim Dormer drove up to her in one of the FBI sedans.

"We just landed a quarter mile down on one of the service roads. I just got off with Graham and Hamlin — they're singing your praises. Hamlin himself said he's going to crucify the MTA prick that allowed the trains to keep running." Dormer looked around. The undercover unit's vehicles were totaled, as well as dump trucks. "You know, not such a bad day's work, all things considered."

"Six agents are dead," she reminded him in a dark tone.

"But no civilian losses or collateral damage."

She stood silent for several seconds before she replied. "Cochrane helped us out. I'm kinda surprised."

"Yeah."

As they walked, Jansen stepped on what was either an oil streak or a thick line of blood.

"What's wrong?"

Jansen just shook her head.

"It's something big," Dormer said, assuredly.

"I've been seeing someone."

"And?"

"How long could this last? The relationship, I mean. It's gonna run into a brick wall because of this job."

"Yeah, it might, if you don't level with him."

"How do you do it?"

"With Eileen?"

"Who else?"

"Well, it ain't easy, but we get by. The problem was always with communication. We couldn't have any kind of communication about my work, she wouldn't understand. That's the big problem of dating out of the job... and dating within the job I guess."

"The guy I'm with — he used to work for the FBI."

"Well, in that case, he probably knows what it's like when shit gets thick. Why did he leave?"

"Politics."

"Hmmm. And I'm guessing you didn't tell him about what you were doing today."

"He's said to me before that it's impossible to be a field agent when there's someone to go home to. There's always that hesitation."

"He's right. But he would also understand the risks better than anyone, and be better prepared — as much as anyone could — if something were to happen. He would get it better than someone like Eileen." The contours on Dormer's face changed when he spoke that last sentence. Jansen noted it. "The best thing you could do is level with him."

Jansen looked off into the distance. The morning sun was yet to ascend above the Verizon building and the other tall structures that stretched from lower to midtown Manhattan. The glass windows on the buildings reflected orange from the early sun into the surrounding areas, giving the city a glowing sheen.

"Are you okay?"

It had occurred to her for the first time, a few moments earlier, that the events leading up to today had been her blooding, and she was now a weathered combatant. Decisively fighting back tears before anyone could notice, she nodded quickly and said, "I will be."

The FBI office was still crowded when Jansen and Dormer returned, but the atmosphere was much lighter. There were people smiling and laughing and there was praise coming from Bill Hamlin.

David Graham went to the interrogation room to release Welles Cochrane. He cleared his throat and held out his hand.

"What you did this morning saved lives. I just wanted to apologize for doubting you. We gotta keep communicating. You know, the Minneapolis thing shouldn't have to happen again."

"Fuck you, Graham. You just lost as big as you gained."

22

Besson was waiting for Jansen outside her apartment. She had called him on her way from the office. Besson had watched the news coverage of the bridge attack all morning and had a preternatural feeling that she was there. He was relieved to hear her voice on the other end of the phone.

She came off the elevator, her eyes red — Besson knew it wasn't from crying. They embraced each other tightly and didn't let go for some time.

"The bridge,"

"I know." Besson said.

They sat on the couch, Jansen sipping steadily from a glass of Southern Comfort.

"I didn't want to tell you that I was going to be stationed there," Jansen explained. "After what you said — about having a relationship and working in a job like this... I just didn't want to think about it."

"But you hesitated anyway."

"Not at first. At the end, one of the suspects made a break for it. I had ducked from fire, and I just stayed on the ground even after I saw him running. It was just for a second or two, but it felt like forever, and before that. One of the units was under heavy fire..."

"And you had to take a life."

"Two lives."

"You really didn't have a choice. You had a job to do — lives were on the line — you had to make a decision and you made the right one."

"I knew what I was doing when I was doing it, and I knew it was the right decision. What scares me is that I didn't hesitate; it was just... reflex. What does that say about me?"

"Nothing. But it says a lot about the world we live in. The rules of engagement have changed, and so has the moral norms. The world has become more complex and morals take a backseat to our objectives. We check our morals at the door."

"Is that part of the oath?" Jansen asked wryly.

"I think it's a recent provision."

"Things used to be different," she reminisced. "It wasn't always like this. It was… simpler, before the Towers fell."

They shared a look of mutual understanding, on the same page for an instant, but lost the flare very quickly. The hull began to press.

She scoffed to herself. "You'd think after hitting the towers there wouldn't be anything else worth hitting besides Kennedy airport."

"It's the famous buildings — symbols of what makes us stand out. The only one left, really, is the Empire State Building. Everyone knows that building, and it's a sign of forward progress."

She buried her face in Besson's chest and wept quietly for a few seconds.

Besson said, "*Lover You Should've Come Over*. The Jeff Buckley cover."

"What?" tears smeared her makeup, lines streaked down her face.

"My favorite song," he confessed

She laughed lightly at the absurdity of it all.

He held her close and kissed her head and at her request they showered together. They caressed each other in the shower, and bathed each other. At one point, Besson moved her sopping hair and whispered something barely audible over the sound of the patting of the water on the tile. It took her a while to figure out what he told her. She later realized he had said "I'm sorry."

Vernon Gibson, free at last — at least until his trial — waited in the alleyway outside of his basement office. It was the dead of night; three a.m. He lit a cigarette and continued to wait patiently, zipping his jacket when the wind blew colder.

Finally, at the beginning of the dead-end alley, he heard the sounds of footsteps and saw a figure shrouded in shadow, carrying a briefcase.

"Gotta tell you, Ms. Dench, you guys are really good. I really thought I was sunk when they were gonna drug me, but the medical records you forged — kick ass."

"Are you sure they didn't suspect anything?" Dench asked.

"I should've won a fucking award. I even pissed my pants and cried. I should charge you extra for that. Speaking of money — is that it there? In the case?"

"Sure is."

"Can I have it now?"

"Go ahead."

Gibson opened the case, and looked through the contents — half a million dollars and a passport.

"I still don't understand why you wanted your buddy to screw up the attack. Don't you guys want to kill Americans and destroy the people that you don't agree with?"

Dench steadied her feet and tensed her legs.

"It's a little bit more complicated than that,"

"Really?"

It was so fast that he didn't even feel it at first. He was looking in the briefcase when she stuck him in a fatty part of his body. The needle was so fine he didn't notice anything until he felt his legs buckle. His breathing erratic, he fell to the floor and clutched his heart until he stopped moving altogether, a look of horror on his face.

Just enough to get the job done, Dench thought, *not enough to show up on an autopsy.*

Into her cell phone, "Now."

Marcus Gardner came down the alley with a rope hidden in his jacket.

"How much did you give him?"

"Enough. Can you make it look good?"

"The pipes are tall enough. It will look fine."

"Great." She quickly dialed her cell phone.

"Yes?"

"Peter, it's Martha."

"And?"

"We've given Mr. Gibson his send off."

"It has to look like a suicide."

"It will."

"Good work. Do not forget about planting the evidence on Ragucci."

"We won't."

"Is everything else working out over there?"

"Besson isn't cooperating very well."

"Don't expect him to."

"When it's over, should we kill him too?"

"No, don't. He hasn't given us a reason to. He believes he's a patriot, trying to save his country from itself. He's a means to our ends. Let him be."

"All right."

"All of you can come home after the installation is complete. After that all we have to do is wait."

"We'll see you soon then."

"Goodbye."

Dench helped Gardner carry Gibson's body back into his office, where she tied the rope around a pipe and wrapped a noose around his neck while Gardner held him up. They balanced his body on the chair Dench had stood on, and let his body drop. When his neck didn't break, Gardner tugged at his legs until he heard a snap.

"Thank you for the help, Mr. Gibson," Gardner muttered.

23

Marcus Gardner met Besson in Brooklyn, outside of the string of apartments that he, Dench and the others had rented. It had been four days since the failed attack on the Manhattan Bridge, and although there was some unrest among the public because they had not been warned, and the casualties may not have been as contained as it was. The Bureau, however, considered it to be a job well done and felt the public's outrage was manageable and would likely blow over soon enough.

"We have a potential security breach."

Besson frowned. "Who?"

"Frank Crowley — the port worker who handled out shipment. We put a tap on his line like you asked, and he's been in contact with the authorities."

"Why is he going to them?"

"He is afraid now that Anderson is dead. He wants to talk to avoid prison."

"Who is he talking to?"

"The Feds are involved."

"Homeland Security?" A likely assumption.

"FBI."

Besson's stomach dropped.

"They've made an appointment to see him *today* outside their office. He's afraid to go in. We need a plan."

"I have one," Besson said quickly. "I need a schematic of the building and the surrounding area, and a few other accoutrements..."

Frank Crowley was pacing nervously just inside the gates outside the FBI building. Jansen and Graham were waiting for him.

The walk up the metal stairways leading to the roof was easy. The two cases were and the bag around his shoulder was heavy but manageable. Besson was in black attire, a knit mask wrapped around his head, ready to be pulled down. He opened the first case, revealing an OSC-5000 Omni-Spectral Correlator, placing a long range Parabolic microphone at the edge of the roof. He found the proper frequency, and hearing Jansen's voice gave him an unsettling pause.

"NYPD is telling us that you may have seen something," Jansen said.

"Mhmm. Yeah."

"Well don't leave us in suspense," Graham replied.

Crowley looked like he hadn't showered in days, and the smell all but confirmed that theory.

"These people came down by the docks and pick up their shipment. It seemed fishy. People don't do this sorta thing."

"Explain."

"Well, the storage containers are usually loaded onto eighteen-wheelers and delivered to whoever."

"And how often would people come to pick their things up?"

"Never that I've seen."

"And how long have you been working there?" Jansen asked.

"Two and a half months, maybe three."

"That's not a very long time. How long have you been with Anderson?"

"Day one."

"And these people he was doing business with — they were suspicious?"

"Well, yeah."

"How?"

"They came in a group, and they drove one of them, uh, vans. The panel vans and the thing they had delivered…"

"What was it?"

"I dunno, but it was in a big, long, wooden box." The words *big* and *long* were emphasized and he looked at Jansen when he said it. "If the C-4 was already in New York, what was the box for? And these people… they didn't work for us. They were people Anderson was doing business with…"

The sniper rifle was placed on a stand, and Besson placed the scope on it. He fiddled with it until it he was able to look down clearly at them. He felt uneasy pointing the weapon in the same small area *she* was in.

"How did these people look and how many were there?" Graham asked.

"Five, six maybe. White. All of them. One woman."

Besson didn't like having to do this.

"Do you have the shipping slip?"

"Yeah, I do."

"We need it."

Besson loaded one bullet into the chamber. He only needed one round.

"Before all that. What do I get in return? For my information."

"The pride in knowing that you helped your fellow Americans."

"I got a record. I want it erased. And some money too, would be nice."

"What charges?"

"It was all bullshit. Nothing really."

Jansen looked through the file.

"What did he do, Andrea?"

"Sexual assaults on two women and accused of raping another."

"I was acquitted."

The trigger became that much easier to pull.

"That doesn't mean two shits—"

A rifle exploded, sounding like a bus starting up. A bullet cut through Crowley's throat and blood gushed out. More spilled on the floor when his convulsing body fell. He was gagging and choking, and Jansen placed her hands over the hole the best she could.

As Graham called for a medic, he spotted a small dark figure on a roof across the street move away. Into his walkie-talkie, "Shooter is in the ware-house, north side quadrant."

Dormer and two other agents were in the warehouse within two and a half minutes. The warehouse was filled with crates, piled at least three on top of each other, held by chains and metal bars. There were thirty rows vertically and horizontally.

"Split up," Dormer ordered.

Besson left the surveillance equipment behind, along with the sniper rifle, and pulled the knit mask down over his face. He threw three smoke bombs down to the floor below and scaled down the metal steps quickly and easily, leaving the bag.

Besson heard coughing in areas far from him as he ran down the rows, going towards the back door, when he was tackled from the side. The air was knocked out of him, his feet were off the ground for half a second, and his back landed hard into the crates behind him. He still had some fight left. Not enough of the smoke had filled the area.

"Come here, mother fucker," Dormer growled.

He landed two punches to Besson's midsection before Besson pushed him away, then grabbed the collars of his jacket, stiffened his knee and pulled Dormer down, catching him in the stomach. Dormer recovered quickly, standing upright. Besson dove at him, pushing him back into another wall of crates. Dormer punched Besson in the face and he moved back. Dormer came forward and boxed again, only to be blocked and met with a stiff punch to the face and another to the head. Besson then grabbed him by his jaw-line and smashed the back of his head into the crate behind him.

Still out of breath and clutching his side, Besson was able to make it through the back door and into the panel truck.

"Are you okay?" Gardner asked.

"I think I cracked a rib. Drive."

Later, Besson changed into new clothes. He threw the other ones into the fire he started in a metal garbage can. Besson wanted very badly to find out if Jansen was all right. He was sure she was. It didn't seem like she had been struck by anything, but he wanted to know for sure. He would have to consult the six o'clock news before he called her.

"Are you sure you don't want Gavin to look at you?"

"I'm fine. How does my face look?"

"A red mark. That's it."

"All right. You'd better get rid of that panel truck."

"I stole the license plate off of some car in a parking lot. The real plates are back at the apartment. I'll replace them."

"We need to deflect any kind of backlash to what we did today," Besson told him.

"Leave that to me. There's a contingency plan in place for this kind of situation."

"I'm sure there is."

"How much longer until we're ready?"

"Not long."

"They're going to be more careful now. This will put them on edge. Hurry up. And you'll have to deter the investigation that they're going to open because of this."

"We'll handle it."

"I hope so," Besson muttered.

Both men looked out from the pier where they were standing. The gray sky had been breached by the setting sun, as it attempted to poke through the darkening clouds. They stood silent for a long moment.

"Do you need a lift back home?" Gardner eventually asked.

"I'll take a cab."

24

Secretary of Defense Alan Kersh received a phone call from FBI Deputy Director Bill Hamlin, who alerted him of the sniper attack at the FBI's New York field office, as well as the possibility of another attack. He set up a meeting with the division heads of the FBI office, himself and the President in the Oval Office.

"What the hell is going on in New York, Al?"

"The FBI office was just hit today. A lone sniper took out a suspect and assaulted three agents before escaping in a panel truck."

"This suspect, why was he hit?"

"He worked for the Port of New York. A few weeks ago, a group of people picked up a suspicious container. Considering most people don't pick up their shipments themselves, and for the fact that *so many* people came to secure this item personally, Frank Crowley — that's his name — called it in. He was being questioned when the sniper struck."

"What leads are they following now?"

"A search of Crowley's home found his phone lines tapped, going to an untraceable source, nearly twenty fetish porn videos, and nothing else worth mentioning. Jim Dormer, one of the field agents who encountered the sniper, said that he was well trained in physical combat, and that his style was reminiscent of defensive styles taught professionally by either the military or any governmental agency — here or abroad."

"Are you saying that we're dealing with somebody domestic?"

"It's hard to say right now, but I wouldn't rule out the possibility."

"What about the shipment? Have they checked the docks?"

"Shipping records indicate the crate that was shipped was large enough to transport a smorgasbord of dirty bombs. They're trying to narrow the list now."

"Tell them to run the worst-case scenarios first, and check for radiation."

"Yes, Mr. President."

"What about the shipping slips?"

"The name on it was Mitchell White. I had Langley run it, and they came up with nothing. Probably an alias."

"Descriptions of suspects?"

"Five or six Caucasians. One woman. That's all we have. We think this is another part to the Anderson attack. The weapons and bullets his people used on the bridge were identical to the ones stolen during the convoy attack where our nuke was stolen. Ballistics matched."

"Are you saying the Sons of Liberty took the bomb, and that it's in New York?" the President asked.

"It's a distinct possibility."

"We're going to have to consider this to be a real threat. I want an interagency protocol enacted between the FBI and Homeland Security, with the FBI running the show."

"Are you sure you want them running things, sir? In a situation like this it would be Homeland Security that has ranking."

"The Bureau handled the Manhattan Bridge attempt well. We should consider taking them in out of the cold. 9/11 was a while ago. I want the same people working on this case also." Ellison paused for a long moment. "I want you to keep the threat level at Blue for the time being, but I want evacuation and martial law scenarios planned out as well as updates from each agency every hour."

"I have the division heads of the FBI field office on the line for you, sir."

"Patch them through."

A flat-panel television screen descended from the ceiling and Kersh stood beside the President. The screen blinked on to the conference room of the FBI field office with all the key personnel, sans Dormer.

"Mr. President," Hamlin began. "I'm Bill Hamlin, Deputy Director of the FBI's CT Division. With me are AD David Graham, SAC Andrea Jansen, Communications Operator Don Walker and Technical Analyst Elizabeth Tess."

"Before we begin, I just want to thank all of you for your exceptional work on the Manhattan Bridge. This country owes all of you a great debt. Now, where are you on this investigation?"

"The bullet we took out of Crowley came from an Accuracy International Super Magnum — very popular in the UK," Tess said. "But you can also pre-order it from several places in the United States. We've worked up a list of people from our side of the pond who've purchased it in the last six months."

"What about the surveillance equipment?" Kersh asked.

"The taps used on Crowley's phone were the same used by the Soviets during the Cold War. It's ex-KGB tech," Walker replied. "The tech that the sniper used is pretty generic. You can even buy it online for a grand or two."

"Have the records of all those websites checked for any purchases of that equipment over the last six months to anyone in the tri-state area," the President ordered. "Cross check it with people on the NCTC list and those with a criminal record. I also wanted to tell you from now: I've enacted an interagency protocol between you, the FBI and Homeland Security — but you will be running the program. All information will pass through your office."

"In that case," Graham prodded. "I would like to ask for some more personnel. We're spread pretty thin as it is, sir."

"Consider it done. Mr. Hamlin, I would like you to return to your office and have your people work in conjunction with the FBI's, and send as many people as Mr. Graham asks for."

"I will, sir."

"Excellent. Secretary Kersh informs me that there is the possibility that we're dealing with an American, or at least an American-trained terrorist. How concrete is that possibility?"

"It's far from confirmed," Jansen said. "Agent Dormer said that only as a description, but, I honestly wouldn't rule anything out right now."

"This sniper, did we get any satellite photos of him?"

"We had no coverage in the area at that time," Tess said.

"Do you have any information on who sent the alleged bomb?"

"The shipping slip claimed that the sender was from Duckford Winery. However, Duckford went out of business thirty years ago and no one bothered to check up on that prior."

Ellison's face was severe. "How likely is it that these two events are connected — the shipping of the C-4 and the bomb."

"We know that Anderson was in charge of the C-4 operation and he went down with the ship," Graham said.

"We can't say that for sure," Jansen interjected. "He very well may have had allies here or abroad."

"Do we know how the C-4 was shipped in the first place?"

"I'm afraid so," Tess replied. She was looking at laptop with a dreadful frown. She turned to Graham and then Ellison. "Several large containers, with a combined weight that adds up to the amount of C-4 we recovered, came into the Port of New York several weeks ago. Duckford Winery was the sender on that shipment too."

"Sweet Jesus," Ellison muttered lowly. "That's basically confirmation then. There's a new threat."

"I'll have Vernon Gibson brought back into custody," Jansen said. "And we should interview some of the Port's staff."

"Don't tell them about Crowley," Graham ordered. "Just tell them he's missing. I want to gauge their reactions."

"Do you suppose it's an inside job?" Kersh asked.

"Two shipments in two months. I'd bet the farm."

"Maybe they just know ports don't have good security," Jansen retorted.

Graham shot her a severe look. The President did also.

There was an uncomfortable silence. She was right, but it didn't help any.

"Have you narrowed down the list of possible contents of that container?" Kersh asked.

"We have, but not by much," Tess said. "There are too many types of dirty bombs and other paraphernalia that could fit the parameters set."

"The military will be sending you the information on the nuclear weapon stolen in September. The FBI DC office has not been able to track it down but we have reason to believe that the nuke could've been in the second container. We need confirmation, or, hopefully, proven unsubstantiated."

"I want the worst-case scenarios worked out first, and bring them to me as soon as possible," Ellison ordered. His look was stoic, but his voice proved his emotions to be contrary to that impression.

The screen went blank and everyone in the FBI office sat silent, the impact of what had just transpired over the preceding few hours.

"We have to stay focused," Hamlin said. "We have to keep fighting to keep this country safe."

His voice seemed prosaic and drained.

Vernon Gibson's apartment was dark, cluttered and smelled stuffy. After a ten-minute intensive search for any clue that he was on the lam, and finding nothing, Jansen headed for Gibson's office.

The assassination of Crowley seemed small in the grander scale of things, Jansen conceded. There could very well be some sort of dirty bomb or God knows what else threatening this country. She wasn't bothered by what happened with the sniper, that she very well could've been killed. She did not fear for herself even as the glass shattered, the haunting noise of Crowley's final gagging breaths, and his mass hitting the floor, gorging blood — the fear she felt belonged to the realization that there was a sequestered design that was now taking center stage. When did her survival become second priority? It's in the oath. But when did she stop *feeling*?

Her hands gripped the steering wheel tightly and her palms began to sweat, but they were not shaking.

The door to Gibson's office was ajar. She drew her Glock, holding it low as she slowly and quietly trekked down the long and dark hallway, her only companion the ubiquitous dripping of the pipes.

Finally, at the arch of the hallway leading into the main office, Jansen hit the switch for the lights.

The sound the rope made as it still continued to tighten around the now leathery skin made a crinkling noise. A chair lay just under the body.

"Oh Christ." Jansen jumped two steps back and her heart dropped. She composed herself quickly and dialed her phone.

"Liz, it's Andrea, I need a Forensic Unit at Vernon Gibson's office. He hung himself."

Graham, the forensic unit and the coroner were on the scene within a half hour. Graham was somewhat surprised that she wasn't waiting outside for them. She was searching the office thoroughly.

"There's nothing here," she said. They watched as the forensic unit cut the noose. "Tell Dr. Parks to run a Toxicology when she gets him."

"Tox test? Why?" Graham asked.

"Suicide doesn't fit into his profile, David. He pissed his pants at the idea of prison time, and he'd be too scared to kill himself."

"Seems he pissed his pants while he was getting hung too. Maybe he thought it was his way to avoid prison altogether."

"Yeah, and maybe he only hung himself just to make it feel better when he jerks off."

"You're fucking morbid sometimes, you know that, Andrea?"

They shared a laugh. For a moment they forgot they were in front of a corpse. Somehow, it made it funnier.

"Maybe the drop didn't kill him," Jansen digressed.

"What are you saying?"

"Maybe Gibson was killed. He was no fanatic. He was a business man. And frankly he wasn't especially valiant." She watched as the body was moved into the black bag.

Graham mulled on the possibility for a second. "It'll be a shitstorm."

The kids had been put to bed awhile ago, and Eileen was angry, and was at the kitchen table, angrily sucking on a Kool cigarette as she sat, waiting to hear the door open, waiting for The Bastard to come home. Hours late at that. The single dinner sitting on the table was cold.

By the time he came home, Eileen had finished her third consecutive Kool. The back of his hair was askew where the staples had been placed. The pain in his head from the fight had been replaced by a different headache, brought by the tapering off of drunkenness.

"Oh Christ, Jim," Eileen moaned. "What... what happened to your head?"

Dormer traced the back of his head gently. "Oh, yeah. That. I, uh, tripped over some files." He said coolly, with only the slightest of slur in his voice.

"Don't make this into a fucking joke, Jim. What happened?"

"I can't go into detail but there was a suspect. And as it turns out, he didn't like being touched."

"Oh, Jesus."

"Oh, but don't worry, Eileen. All it took was a few staples to stop the bleeding, and the concussion isn't so bad."

"Don't be cute. You've been drinking — I can smell it from here."

"I had a few, but I'm fine. So what?"

"Did they give you meds?"

"Yeah—"

"And you're out getting drunk! Good, Jim, real good. You don't take the time to care about yourself. I never know what's going on with you — you're never on time for dinner, the girls never see you anymore, you come home all hours of the day and night —and I never know when, you could be dead for all I know..."

"Don't be so fucking dramatic, Eileen." A pause. "You've been drinking too, haven't you?"

"Don't be dramatic?! Look at you! You're beaten up and you're fucking drunk."

"For Christ's sake Eileen, shut the fuck up before you wake the girls!"

"Fuck you, Jim. When was the last time you even saw them? Did you know Meagan is failing Social Studies? The teacher said she's not doing her homework and she's *acting out*. Who could blame her when she has an absentee father?"

"It's almost as bad as having a cunt for a mother."

Eileen's eyes widened, she slapped him with both hands. "Mother fuck-er… I can't fucking do this anymore, Jim. Things have to change or…"

"I know."

The girls were watching from their rooms, their faces like stone. It was a typical night in the Dormer household.

A thumb of Southern Comfort in a tumbler, downed, reloaded, and downed again. Jansen changed into her sweats, and let her hair out of her ponytail. She fell onto the couch, reloaded the tumbler and turned on the television. She rubbed her feet, which ached to hell, and downed the SoCo. She grabbed her phone once the booze warmed her.

Besson's heart skipped a beat and his body jumped when the phone rang — which made his rib hurt as his body twitched — and then slowed to a normal beat for the first time all day once he saw Andrea's name flash-ing on the screen on his cell phone. His hello was casual and nondescript.

"Hey, Will."

"What's going on?"

"Not much, I just got home from work."

"You sound beat."

"It was a long day."

"Anything worth mentioning?" Besson knew the difference between being able to talk and not. It often comes down to wanting to talk; in her case, it was a little of both that kept her from telling the truth.

"Not really."

"Is there anything I can do?"

"No, but it's good to hear your voice."

Besson drew a breath to say something. She heard this and waited, but nothing ever came.

"I'll talk to you tomorrow," Jansen quickly promised.

"Have a good night."

"You too. Take care."

"Yeah, you too."

25

It always happened the same way: The El Paso shooting of Manolo Cervantes — a mid-level drug dealer trying to make a name for himself by doing business with a known al-Qaida associate. The raid. Son of a bitch took his own son hostage. No time to wait for a negotiator. Tried himself. Cervantes let the boy go. Besson emptied a clip in him.

Eight days passed. He awaited the Shooting Review Board; the customary investigative measure taken whenever an agent fires his or her service weapon, on or off duty.

Andrea Jansen was questioned, as well as Carl McDowell and BAU Section Chief Paul Sullivan, in order to get an idea of Besson's psychological profile and professional and personal demeanor. Finally, Besson himself was called into the room. He walked in awkwardly, his hip wound throbbing and burning.

The room was large and dark. It had a large window, but little light came through the venetian blinds on that cloudy day. Besson dismissed the irony. He sat at a small black desk facing all top Bureau's top assistant directors as well as the deputy director and a representative from the Department of Justice. Most of them were there out of inclination. Only a few had ever met Besson and actually knew him. All of them, however, were above the age of forty-five, and they all had aged, dour faces and dead eyes.

They all sat in a row, perched atop a long glossy panel, the FBI emblem at its center. The FBI seemed so tired to Besson at that moment. It was so unable to function it was attacking one of its own members in its own incompetence.

Deputy Director Diana Pierce of the Office of Professional Responsibility began the hearing, summing up what had been said by the other people that were questioned.

"Agent Besson, from the looks of this last report and from your record, despite your obvious acumen and care for your work in the BAU and the CTD there are certain... *stains* on your record which impede your case," she said.

"Such as?" he asked.

"Your lack of discipline as far as a dress code — when you captured Ludlow Kealty reporters took pictures of you in casual clothes, which you seem to wear often to the office. Also, Section Chief Paul Sullivan has remarked on your record and to this committee that you have a problem with authority and often question orders." Pierce's quiet voice did not negate her strong belief in what she said, and her voice had grown more agitated as she listed the grievances against Besson.

"I only question my orders because I try to do what's best to get my cases solved as quickly as possible and save more lives... and Paul, well he and I don't get along because I wouldn't be his yes-man jellyfish."

"We do not appreciate your tone, agent."

"Your job is to follow orders, not to question them," Crosby, the DOJ representative, said.

"Accepted. But you cannot honestly expect me to take the dress code grievance seriously."

"You should, Agent Besson." Keeler said; Office of Professional Conduct.

"Fine, but let me just tell you, a lot of times I'm in the field and it's better to talk to witnesses that feel comfortable around you and feel like their talking to one of their friends rather than a *G-man* in a black and white suit. We're likely to get more accurate information quicker if the people I talk to feel comfortable around me."

"Is it supposed to make them feel comfortable, or you?" Pierce asked. "We're the FBI. We're here to do a job, not coddle."

"Hold on a moment," Harris intervened. He was a friend of Besson's, and the rare luxury on the Career Board. "This is about a shooting, not about proper garments."

"Indeed," Pierce said. "We are here because Mr. Besson *took* a life, not because he wore jeans doing it," she said dryly.

Mr. Besson. Pierce has already decided what they're going to do to me. This whole show is just a pretense; something for the records, Besson thought. Paul and Diana finally got their chance to flush me. "And I saved the life of a young boy in the process," Besson replied in a deep, emphasizing tone.

The room stood quiet for a moment. "Your report described what happened at the shooting," Pierce finally said. "You found the hostage and Manolo Cervantes, and he opened fire on you."

"That's right."

"Then Cervantes ran out of bullets, correct?" Crosby asked.

"Correct." There was a lump in his throat.

"And you killed him anyway, in cold blood?" Keeler asked, with a hint of disgust.

"Yes," Besson said softly.

"Why did you shoot Mr. Cervantes then? He obviously was no threat to you."

"Was he still a threat to the boy?" Harris asked.

He could have lied then, could have gotten away with it. Besson opted instead to tell the truth. To this day he never understood why he did it. Perhaps it was his natural inclination. Maybe he wanted to make a point. Or, in some strange way, he knew that despite what he said there was no way to get around the fact that his career was ending and there was no reason to leave on anything else but his own terms. There was a certain nobility to it — at least the way he saw it.

"After Cervantes realized he had no more bullets, he dropped the gun and let the boy go."

"What happened then?" Harris asked.

"He raised his hands over his head, and…" Besson trailed off. "It's in the report."

"Cervantes raised his arms in the air, and you shot him seven times, killing him in cold blood," Crosby coldly accused.

"Yes." His voice faltered.

"You are away of the Bureau's deadly force policy, aren't you?"

"Yes I am."

"Then why did you pull the trigger?"

"The world won't grieve now that he's not in it. We're better off with him dead," Besson calmly said.

"That wasn't your decision to make," Pierce reminded him.

"It was a judgment call. I carry a badge and gun with the promise that I would use my best judgment. I had to make a decision right then and there, and I still stand by that decision now."

"This kind of cold-blooded action is not tolerated in the FBI; you should know this by now," Harris said.

Someone muttered, "Gangbuster."

The room seemed to teeter on the edge, scared silent, as if a single word could trigger an avalanche. Pierce dared the mountains to quake. "Having a badge and gun doesn't give you a license to kill. You have no right to choose who lives and who dies. The FBI is a proud institution, Mr. Besson. These actions will not be tolerated."

Above the row of assistant directors was the symbol of the FBI which seemed so tired and insignificant. The Bureau was an aged agency and, not unlike an old man, it was not able to adapt to the rapidly changing times. The world was becoming much more complicated and dangerous, and to Besson's belief, the FBI should change with the times, and react with greater force to compensate and adapt to the changes.

The last thing Besson remembered was hearing Agent Pierce telling him there would be another meeting tomorrow morning. Besson was surprised by their speed. He exited the room and put on his sunglasses in spite of the cloudy day. He was a dead man, no doubt.

He walked out to the parking lot and was completely numb to the world around him. Not far from him, Andrea Jansen saw him and walked towards him.

"How did it go in there?"

"If they had three nails, they could've crucified me on the FBI emblem."

Besson sat in front of the board for a second time, four days later. This was a follow-up of the Shooting Review Board, which concluded that Agent Besson needed to be reprimanded; but not have charges put against him. It sounded like he was under duress and likely needed a long vacation. Of course, they needed to be sure. The proper procedures had to be followed.

Besson noticed Carl McDowell and Paul Sullivan sitting outside of the office, waiting. Besson and McDowell nodded to each other. Sullivan glared.

Inside:

"Do you believe that shooting Manolo Cervantes was an action taken without judgment, that it is an action you feel, in hindsight, was wrong?" Pierce asked Besson.

Besson hesitated a moment, and thought it over one last time, "No."

"Then we have no choice then to suspend you indefinitely while the Justice Department conducts a formal investigation, and ask you to take part in a psychological competency exam. If you do not comply or fail the test, you will be disbarred."

"That's a bad call," Besson retorted.

"And it isn't your call to make, *Agent* Besson. I doubt I must remind you, that it is the authority the agency that you've so adamantly claimed to defend which makes *that call*," Pierce said. Her voice was pointed; taking a joyful allocation in Besson's dishonor.

"Because of me there's one less drug dealer corrupting *our* children. Because of *me*, the cartel has one less leader. What *you're* doing is wrong." In a growing tone, "You know I'm mentally competent, and deep down you're all happy I capped Cervantes. If any of you have ever seen someone you believed should be **killed**, then you're as guilty as I am. Punishing me for this is hypocritical. The Bureau needs to change with the times."

"It's outbursts like **that** didn't do much to plead your case," Pierce said. "You haven't given us **much** of a choice. Comply or be disbarred."

The speed of the Board in making a decision that had originally stunned Besson now made sense. The Board had every intention of flushing him in the first place; that Besson's first instinct had been correct. The meetings were just a formality, something for the records — which probably also explained the fact that the Employee Assistance Program hadn't reached out to him, and why he was brought in front of OPR and the Career Board so promptly. The reason they responded quickly — beyond that of the flushing — was so the initial incident would still be at the forefront of people's minds in and out of the Bureau; he wouldn't be brought up on charges because this was his punishment. He was set to be the first martyr of the Zero Tolerance policy that Director Bowman had enacted.

"We all know that I wasn't here to plead my case. It was requisite for the sake of reports. So I'll save you all the trouble. I quit." Besson said angrily. He threw his badge down on the table, then slowly shuffled out of the room, and all the while couldn't bring himself to look at McDowell or Sullivan directly in their eyes.

The aphorism of the FBI burned into his mind. "Fidelity, Bravery, Integrity."

Reflecting now, Besson felt as if those red-letter days happened a lifetime ago, though he couldn't help but recall each moment with the same precision as if it happened just the moment before. Soon, another day would stake its claim, burning into his memory its events and its invariable changes. It was then that Besson wondered if his memory would be the Hell he would eventually face.

26

When she got off the phone with Lavalle, Martha Dench was ecstatic. After today's work was over, she and the rest of the cell would be returning home on an afternoon flight. Their nearly eight-month excursion was coming to a close; all that was left was the installation.

Gardner arrived in a Red Sun van; his orders were followed implicitly.

Besson had told them that they would plant the bomb in a building in midtown Manhattan. Considering the near impossibility of hiding it in such an important building — one with a high likelihood of attack — Besson told Lavalle that he would need the proper attire and identification of one who worked for a heating company so he could smuggle the bomb in under the guise that it was a new boiler or heater. Lavalle had complied, to an extent, and although Besson didn't want to admit it — as it would undermine his own dominion — Lavalle's changes were well thought out and superior to his original plan.

Marcus Gardner had been in the employ of Red Sun Heating during this past summer and by now had become a trusted employee. During the last check of the boilers at the targeted building, Gardner made sure not to log in his report that one boiler was going to have to be replaced within six months. It had, just recently, and a call to Red Sun was made to replace it.

Showing up to work early, Gardner had been selected to replace the boiler. He disassembled it, so only the shell remained intact. The bomb would fit perfectly inside. He would then tell the janitor in charge of the boiler room — Salvatore Dante — that a necessary conduit was missing and that Red Sun would have to special order it and that it wouldn't come until after the holidays; and since the bomb would still be insulated, the janitorial staff wouldn't be effected by the radiation and wouldn't give them anything else to worry about. Gardner would tell Red Sun that the installation of the new boiler was successful and hand in his resignation at the same time. It would all have to run like clockwork.

Besson arrived at the warehouse that the sleeper cell had housed the bomb and found everyone was set.

"Is the bomb working?"

"We activated it just now," Gardner said. He handed Besson the PDA Dr. Grey had reworked. "Dr. Grey has it set so that a pass code would have to be entered at the twelve, six and one hour marks on the day of in order for it to detonate."

"Why?"

"It was part of the security system that she wasn't able to augment. The code is zero-seven-four-seven-six. If you don't enter the code in for those three check points the bomb will shut itself down and the PDA won't be able to turn it back on. The only other way to detonate it would be manually, and that isn't something you want."

"Can't argue with that,"

"I took the liberty of getting you the same uniform as the rest of us from Red Sun, as well as some ID's. There was also something else in the crate besides the bomb that I believe is yours."

Gavin, the medic, handed Gardner a black suitcase, which he opened, revealing the twelve million Besson asked for up front. Besson nodded, and closed it. The handle had a tag on it which read:

TO: THE HARBINGER
FROM: P.L. & M.F.S.

"Do you know what it means?" Gardner asked, confused.

"Yeah," Besson muttered indignantly. *Lavalle the Wry.*

Gardner drove the van while the others remained in the back, motionless and quiet. Besson watched the skyline, gazing and waiting.

"Let me ask you something," Dench said. "Don't you think you could've picked a safer place to hide to bomb until its detonation?"

"No," Besson replied. "The best place to hide something is in plain sight and they won't look where we're putting it."

"Still. Why?"

"Because it's in the center of midtown, and when the government figures out that another beacon of New York was the epicenter, it will supplement the message."

"How poetic," Dench replied sarcastically.

"Just keep your head in the game. We're here."

Dench turned and peered from the windshield at the target building. The beacon that he had been talking about. The epicenter. The Empire State building.

Security let them through without any hassle, and they wheeled the bomb down into the boiler room via a small stairwell.

Sal Dante, head of maintenance, remained sequestered in his corner, waiting for the intruders to leave. He waited the requisite time needed to install a new boiler and came to check on them.

"You done yet?" he gave his best effort to sound like he came from a *Soprano's* call sheet.

"Yes we are." Gardner replied. "You wouldn't happen to have an extra circulating pump down here, would you?"

"No."

"Shit. I don't have one with me in the van, and the office said we're all out. Let me call our suppliers." Gardner talked to no one on his cell phone for almost two minutes. Besson was impressed by his act. Finally, "I'm sorry to tell you, Mr. Dante, that our suppliers won't be able to send us the pump until sometime after Christmas."

"I can't wait that long. They're breakin my balls over this already. I'll order it myself."

"Don't worry about it. We'll take care of it," Besson offered. "and because of the mix up, we won't charge you for it."

Dante nodded grudgingly. "Fine, but there's something else you could do too,"

"What's that?" Dench asked, piqued.

"Explain it to my boss so he doesn't blame it on me."

Gardner smirked. "Sure."

Later, back in the van and driving away from the Empire State building, the tone was much lighter now that the mission was completed and almost everyone in the van were going home. Besson remained stoic, and reserved.

"What's wrong, Besson?" Dench asked. "Aren't you relieved?"

"No."

"Why?"

"Because it isn't over yet. I'll be relieved when it's over."

He looked out and into the Manhattan skyline again, looking at the sun beating down, brilliantly and vividly. Besson wondered what it would look like on Christmas Eve when the island burns up brighter than the sun. The irony of it all; the country's darkest hour would be found in a blinding light of a thousand suns.

He decided then what it would look like: a ballad of the fallen.

27

December; Crawford, Philadelphia

The way the passage of time affects the body, running it ragged, is particularly cruel.

Pushing sixty, bad knees and, as it turned out, a medical condition. The doctor they had on staff at the prison was an asshole. He knew what was wrong and he sat on it. Out of spite. Passing judgment. He told the guards, got an audience with the warden about his chest pains.

"Just gas," he was told mockingly.

"Getting older, body slowing down," the cocksucker doctor said.

When he collapsed in his cell, that turned heads. The doctor — that fucker — was on vacation and they had to medivac him to the nearest hospital. In Crawford.

If he was anybody else, he would've been given fair treatment. Even as an inmate. If he wasn't Ludlow Kealty. If he wasn't the Somerton Hangman, who'd raped, tortured and hung twelve women in Somerton over a nearly twenty-year-long rampage. He had a correspondence with the local and eventually federal authorities — writing poems and letters about his kills. Looking back, they were his glory days. Especially those last two years when the FBI agents were brought in from DC. They did the cat-and-mouse thing before finally catching him in — at least in Kealty's opinion — an excessively humiliating way: traced him through an email account from the internet café he frequented, and arrested him while he was attending mass with his wife.

Because of those two cocksuckers from Washington, his wife killed herself and his kids won't talk to him. Won't even let him see his grandkids. The truth always pops up when you least want it. The same could be said about medical problems. His prognosis was bad: lung cancer, a doctor finally told him. Beginning stage four, he said, before leaving the room. He almost seemed glad to see him in this condition. Son of a bitch. If he had enough strength he would've bitten the doctor's throat out.

The sunlight that came through the Venetian blinds was enough to divert his ire. He saw hints of the sky through them — first time he had seen it in four years, since being in solitary after a run-in with another inmate.

Realizing how a choppy view of the sky was an abject treat made his situation that much more pathetic and embittering.

As the monitors beside him beeped rhythmically, recording heart rate, another helped his breathing — tubes sticking out of his nose.

Through the square window in the door he caught Carl McDowell passing by, sipping a coffee.

With all the time he had on his hands in solitary confinement, Kealty spent the majority of it reading. Newspapers, articles online — on the few occasions he was actually granted access (and in-between watching bondage porn) — he read up on his favorite FBI agents. He had learned of the public shaming and eventual dismissal of Agent Besson, though the reverberations of his actions were wider in scope. Those close to him in the Bureau became scorched earth — guilty by association (not unlike his family had been following his incarceration: Kealty read that own his children changed their surnames after his conviction). From what he read, Agent Jansen had escaped a great deal of wrath by transferring out of the DC office, but Besson's partner wasn't as lucky. Carl McDowell stayed in DC and didn't ask for a transfer from the BAU. For that he paid through the teeth. It was hard enough being an African American in the FBI, but because of the Besson incident, McDowell's career suffered for quite some time. He was passed over for Section Chief in favor of some hotshot from John Jay College.

These two men were never far from Kealty's mind, and would even find himself aroused when dreaming of the ways in which he would pay them back if he could. Now, the opportunity presented itself. Kealty was a dead man anyway, and he had no qualms about dying. Better than the way he was living nowadays.

Ideas moved along slowly, liking driving through mud. He noticed his right hand was cuffed to the sidebar attached to the bed, and peering through the square window in the door he saw McDowell still pacing outside in the corridor continually. The cuff, which was likely attached or reattached by some half-witted nurse or security guard, was connected to the metal sidebar on the lowest rung, where the sidebar connected to the bed. All he had to do was detach the sidebar, and the cuff would no longer encircle it.

Kealty smiled.

He slowly pulled the machine that monitored his vitals and heartbeats with his free hand. He pressed the alarm button, shutting down the possibility of the monitors compromising his position. He took the tubes out of his body grudgingly, and turned his attention to the sidebar he was cuffed to. As he sat up, blood rushed from his head, the Oxycontin and the antibiotics making him dizzy. The room was spinning.

Come on. Focus. Breathe deep, he thought to himself.

He detached the bar slowly, so as not to make a sound. The cuff slipped off once the sidebar detached, and Kealty held it as long as he could. His muscles loosened and the bar became that much easier to hold.

Unable to totally rationalize yet, he was still only able to recall bits and pieces, like an alcoholic pulling at vague strings after waking up with a severe hangover. McDowell was outside in the corridor. McDowell. He felt the sun beating down through the windows, hot on his back. Today was the first day in years that he had seen or felt sunlight. Son of a bitch darkie cop.

Above Kealty's bed was an emergency alarm nurses press in case a doctor was needed in an emergency; usually if a patient needs to be resuscitated. Kealty slammed the button for the alarm, and a siren went off.

His head was spinning, the siren enough to make his ears bleed. They might actually be. He could get away in the middle of all of this chaos. Beat McDowell. Steal his gun and keys. Go to the parking lot and steal his car.

Intuitively, McDowell burst through the door of Kealty's room, only to be met by the metal sidebar, slammed deep into his abdomen. He fell back against the wall, coughing. Kealty's arms were shaking and he could no longer bear holding the sidebar.

"How does it feel to be denied breath, you fuck." A hoarse Kealty grabbed the Glock from McDowell's shoulder holster and pressed it to his stomach. "The tragic irony."

For a single moment, the sound of the alarms was drowned by a barely muffled gunshot. Staff members who were swarming toward the corridor, all turned around; patients ran from their rooms. Security was on its way.

Kealty attempted to run from the room; his legs, weakened from the drugs fighting in his system, coughing and having trouble breathing — dizzy now. His legs buckled and he fell outside, as fearful patients and staff members ran scared. A security guard ran towards him, and Kealty blew a hole in the guard's chest. The force of it almost made him fall. He was able to grasp the wall, which he now needed to help him bound slowly across the hall.

Despite the hot blood pouring from his belly and the internal wounds he likely incurred, Carl McDowell's resolve remained strong. He was running on instinct, his hand covering the gunshot wound. With the other, he reached down to his legs which were damp — was it blood? sweat?—and they were shaking badly. He moved his legs towards his free arm, hurting like hell, but he reached the Walther PPK he kept at his ankle. He turned over on his stomach, one hand still holding the wound, the other dragging him to the outside corridor. His legs were shaking too much for him to stand, let alone walk. This was as fast as he was going to move. McDowell had made it out of the room in enough time to see Kealty blast the guard and make his way back up. Kealty was making strides, holding his hand to the wall as he walked.

"Ludlow!" McDowell called weakly.

Kealty kept moving.

McDowell was slipping into shock. No time. No choice. Take the shot and make it count.

Another deafening blast and Kealty held his thigh as it gushed with blood. He let out a stricken yelp, and fell, defeated, like a deer caught by a veiled hunter. He continued to yell and was rolling on the floor, stopping when he caught McDowell's gaze.

Slipping deeper into shock, and the loss of blood making things cold and blurry, McDowell made a decision. Kealty already knew what it was. Better it happen this way than in a hospital bed alone on a respirator.

It seemed to happen in slow motion: Kealty attempting to find his gun, not taking his eyes from McDowell's. Security guards were running towards the corridor, which was full of smoke, the floor streaked in blood and smelling of gunpowder. There was a concluding and unanswerable blast followed by a unitary silence. No alarms or gunshots. Nothing. A small, uneven, circular hole in Kealty's forehead bled in one thin line down his face.

The last thing McDowell saw before slipping into the bottomless chasm was Kealty's gape, blank and wide, like a deer caught in the headlights.

28

Manhattan, New York

Since returning to New York, Besson watched the news incessantly, looking for any sign that someone had found something detrimental to his mission. Nothing had come as yet. He changed from the Fox News Channel back to CNN, and in a moment of sheer horror, saw an enlarged picture of Ludlow Kealty on the screen. His heart skipped a beat, and the nape of his neck was hot. The picture of Kealty disappeared and was replaced by Carl McDowell's, and Besson heard the entire saga of what happened at the hospital-turned-war zone, how the revered, wounded and lone FBI agent prevented the escape of one of America's worst serial killers.

Besson was to his feet, and on the phone to the FBI. The secretary on the switchboard patched him through to Assistant Director Ronald Harris's cell phone, which, judging from the sounds in the background was on a plane.

"This is Harris."

"Ron, it's Will."

"Who?"

"Besson. Will Besson. What the fuck is going on over there, Ron?"

Harris knew immediately what he was talking about.

"Kealty had taken ill and was moved to a civilian hospital. The new Section Chief had Carl go to make sure things didn't go wrong. He figured Carl's prior experience with Kealty would keep him from pulling any shit. Kealty woke up and broke from his restraints. He attacked Carl, and Carl blasted a hole through his head. Kealty's dead, and Carl is in a bad way. I'm flying over to the hospital now to see him."

"What's the name of the hospital?"

"St. Francis in Crawford, Philadelphia."

"I'm on my way."

Besson hung up before Harris could retort. Harris sighed aloud, looked at his watch, and mixed an Alka-Seltzer.

Besson called Jansen and left her a voicemail explaining the situation, and apologizing for his breaking of the date they had scheduled. He promised to call her once things settled. She called him back just as he turned onto the highway.

"I heard on the news," she said. "If I can, do you want me to follow you?"

"No, it's okay. I'm not sure how long I'll be gone for."

"I'm so sorry, Will."

"I'll talk to you later."

Besson hung up, and refocused on the road. His eyes were moist and narrow, and he felt angry, on the verge of violence.

It was early in the evening when Besson made it to the hospital. Ronald Harris was standing outside McDowell's room, disheveled and tired.

"Will," he began.

"How is he?"

"That's what I gotta talk to you about."

Besson pushed passed him, trying to get into the room. Harris pushed him back.

"He's not in there anymore. Listen to me, Will. I'm sorry..."

"No," Besson growled defiantly, knowing what Harris was going to say, but not ready to accept it.

"The doctors couldn't stop the internal bleeding... he passed about a few hours ago."

Besson collapsed into the chair by the door and barely choked out, "How did he do it? How did Kealty..." He couldn't bring himself to say it, to admit it.

"The cuff that was attached to the sidebar on the bed was put on the last rung. He slipped it off. Some dipshit nurse put it on wrong after they took him for an X-ray."

Besson's head was down, his face in his hands.

"I just talked to Annette. The funeral is going to be in two days, back in DC. She said it would mean a lot to her and Brian if you showed up."

"I'll be there," he whispered.

"Do you need anything, Will?"

"No, no. You can go. I just need to sit for minute."

"All right. I'll see you in DC. Call if you need anything."

Besson nodded solemnly.

"Are you okay?" a little girl's voice called from the room across from him.

Besson peered in and saw a girl, no older than ten, in a hospital bed. She had tubes and monitors around her, and an oxygen mask over her mouth.

"You seem sad," the girl said.

Besson walked into the room slowly.

"A friend mine... I just lost a friend of mine."

"I'm sorry."

"It's not your fault," he said stagnantly.

"My name's Sarah." Her spacing between words was elongated due to the pumping of the oxygen mask. Her voice was weak and slow.

"Will."

"Are you a cop?"

"No, not anymore."

"Oh. You look like a cop."

"Why are you here?" he asked, ignoring the irony of her comment.

"They say I have a problem with my heart,"

Besson peeked at her chart, seeing such terms as: SURGERY UN-SUCESSFUL and FAILURE IMMINENT and felt guilty for mentioning death earlier in their conversation, partnered with a sincere sadness for her.

"I've had this all my life," she said.

"Where are your parents?"

"I don't have any. I live in a shelter for other kids without mommies and daddies."

"I'm sorry," Besson said, standing at her bedside.

A single tear ran down her face.

"What about friends?" he asked.

"I never had any because I got sick always. I couldn't play with them a lot."

Besson looked around for any cards or dolls and found none.

"You know, I didn't get to have a childhood either."

"Really?"

"Mhmm."

Sarah's breathing became erratic, and the machine's began to beep. She sounded as if she was struggling. When Besson went to get someone she told him not to. Her breathing returned to normal soon after.

"This happens a lot. I'm okay now. What happened when you were a kid?"

"I lost my parents when I was your age too."

"It hurts… losing your family."

"Yes it does."

"I wish I knew who my parents were."

"I'm sure they loved you."

"Then why didn't they want me?" Her voice was sullen and desperate, begging for an answer no one could give her.

"Well, they probably thought they were doing what's best for you."

"Does the pain ever go away, Will?" she said after spending several seconds seemingly lost in thought.

Besson's throat was tight and his chest felt heavy. He was barely able to choke out a white lie, saying, "Yes."

"That's good." Sarah had another attack, this one longer than the last. "I know I'm gonna die," she said afterwards.

"Don't say that."

"I heard the doctors saying so." She paused, stopping herself from saying something.

"What is it?"

"Can you stay with me, Will? I'm scared."

Besson nodded, and sat in the chair beside her bed. He offered her hand which she held as tightly as her small fingers would allow her. Through the course of the night, their hands remained melded, and as the night drew on into the early morning, Besson felt her already weak grip begin to loosen and her hand grow cold. When the machine signaled a flat line, he turned it off and placed her hand back onto the bed. He kissed her on the cheek. He shuffled outside the hospital, not bothering to hide the tears that were streaming from his eyes.

In the short time that she had been alive, Sarah had known only loneliness, alienation and seclusion. She knew nothing of a warm home and affectionate family, a comforting bed and the distinctive love than can only come from a parent.

The only records of her existence would be the certificates of her birth and death. These certificates, however, would not detail that in her final hours she had known the same love and kindness that had eluded her throughout her short life.

She learned that it was never too late to learn what love was and what it was like to make an impact on someone; that although she had gone through life alone, she learned it didn't have to end the same way.

Due to his extended stay at the hospital, Besson wouldn't make it in time for McDowell's wake, but he would make it for the funeral. Leaving his Altima in the short-term parking lot, he chartered a flight.

He took a cab from the airport and rented a suit for the funeral. Once at a hotel, he called Annette, McDowell's wife of twenty-odd years, and spoke to her briefly, so he could give her his condolences. She thanked him, and asked if he would be one of the pallbearers. Besson told her he would be honored.

Sufficiently tired because of the flight and the conversation, Besson showered and watched the news. He picked up his phone at one point to call Andrea. He dialed the number, but didn't press SEND.

The Mass was held in a cathedral-like church in Georgetown. The turn-out was immense, with people from the FBI, local police, and the Marines. Carl was always much better at handling people than Besson was. He could rally men behind him. He was easily and quickly loved by the people who met him.

Diana Pierce and the now-retired Paul Sullivan were there as well. Besson locked eyes with them and contemptuous stares were exchanged.

Annette asked that Besson sit up front with the family during the Mass and at the burial. He agreed, and realized just how easily he had forgotten how close McDowell and he were. He was stricken by a wave of guilt.

The procession took the mourners through the neighborhood McDowell grew up in, as well as Quantico.

At the burial ceremony at Arlington cemetery, Besson sat with Annette and McDowell's only son, Brian, who was on leave from a tour of duty. Tears welled in his eyes. Besson watched Annette's lined face, eyes gleaming, her gaze never faltering from that of the coffin. She held hands with him and Brian throughout.

The presiding minister continued his sermon as the coffin sank slowly into the earth. It was then that the tombstone came slowly into view. Below that of McDowell's name, along with the years of his birth and death, the tombstone read a quote from Wilfred Owens: "Dulce Et Decorum Est," *sweet and fitting it is to die for one's country.*

The coffin disappeared and the Marines fired their rifles in salute, and Besson realized, for the first time since hearing the news, what exactly had happened. His throat tightened and he felt heaviness in his chest.

Annette took a handful of soil in her hand and sprinkled it onto the top of the coffin. Not everything that returns to the earth is sent there to be reborn.

In the Bureau, families are offered lectures for dealing with this kind of occasion, if you get that unwelcome phone call. They tell you that its part of the oath your loved-one took, that their sacrifice would never be in vain. They teach you the best ways in which to prepare yourself in the event of this kind of loss. However, what they can never teach you, what they can never prepare you for, is how much it hurts — every single day.

For people like Carl McDowell, Will Besson, and countless other men, the job is haunted. Their conviction to this idea could be found in their regrets of the pride they had to swallow, the eating away at — and eventual loss of — their morals, taking with it all personal hopes and mandates; all in the name of something higher than themselves. In truth, it is not the job that is haunted, it's the men who are haunted.

It was late at night when Besson returned to New York. At a red light, he stared out the window, seeing the Empire State Building.

Each peak at the top floors of the building had a different color. From the top spire there was red, the two subsequent summits white, then blue. Those lights bounced off from the mist and the drizzle in the air, perceiving as if the building was smoldering and steaming, on the verge of scorching.

Besson looked away quickly and stared intently at his steering wheel. The dream he had flashed in his mind, as he looked up to the building again, rapt by its unnatural visage.

29

Graham was sitting in the conference room. He had taken two Tramadol to compliment the Valium he took this morning. When everyone was finally seated in the room, Graham drew a long breath, and said, "Where are we on finding the sniper?"

There was an uncomfortable silence.

"Are you fucking kidding me?"

"We have nothing," Jansen said. "Whoever is masterminding this did so by using items that are essentially untraceable."

"What about the records from websites that were carrying the surveillance tech and the sniper rifle."

"I'm going through the lists, but not too many of the people are fitting are parameters," Tess said.

"Widen your search."

"Sir, we also have a new wrinkle," Walker announced. "I heard from our source at the *Post* that they're releasing a story about the sniper hit at the office."

"Oh, Christ." Graham sighed. "What are they saying?"

"That the attack could be a prelude to another Oklahoma City."

"The *Post* is nothing more than a glorified tabloid. We should be able to discredit them pretty easily," Jansen said.

"But their audience is large. Don, I want you to plant a story with our friends at the *New York Times* and the *Wall Street Journal*. Tell them that it was a nut — like Timothy McVeigh, they'll like that — and that he was captured..."

"Sir, McVeigh carried out the Oklahoma City bombing."

"Then give them the name of some whacko fucking postman. Tell them that no one from the office was hurt or killed and that the sniper's identity will be revealed in due course." Graham took several deep breaths, as if the speech had winded him. "Did Dr. Parks get back to us on the Toxicology test for Gibson?"

Jansen peeked at the file in front of her. "There was an elevation in his epinephrine levels before he died, which could mean he was fighting hard to get away from the noose, but…"

"What?"

"His medical records say that he has a heart problem and the amount of epinephrine in his system was enough to make his heart literally beat to death. Autopsy also shows that his neck was broken post mortem."

"So it could've been murder, but it also could've been a suicide that just happened differently than he expected."

"It's still unclear."

"Find out. We need to find the real sniper and whoever else may be involved in this case. The holidays are coming up, so something is going to happen — probably within the next two weeks. We need to stop it before it happens. Dismissed."

Warren Ragucci's cramped apartment in Astoria was a mess, and its only source of light came from windows which were blotted out by curtains.

Jansen and Dormer tossed every inch of the apartment for over an hour. The mattress, couch and pillows were cut open, his computer was searched and taken apart, and his desk was searched. They even took his stereo system and television apart.

"Find anything?" Jansen asked.

"Nothing."

They regrouped in the living room and readied themselves to leave. Dormer stared at the wall by the door, somewhat perplexed.

"What is it?" Jansen asked.

"Open the curtains."

The light came into the room and brightened the area.

"Look at that on the wall. There's a small area that's painted darker than the rest of the wall."

"Maybe there was a hole in the wall."

"Maybe." Dormer walked over to it the patch and touched it. "There was some leftover drywall that was cut that I found in the bedroom."

"And?"

"The other walls in this apartment don't have dry wall in them."

Dormer smashed the patch with his elbow, breaking through the dry wall and discovering a small tape recorder. He pulled it out and pressed PLAY.

The content of the tape was of a telephone conversation between Dr. Moira Grey — the still unknown woman with a British brogue — and Warren Ragucci. The conversation became a point of interest once it started to answer questions:

"Your boss is a high-probability target once the attack succeeds. If captured he will turn on us. You can take his share plus another twenty thousand if you kill him when it's over."

"Fifty."

"Thirty-five."

"Fine."

"We're at an understanding then. We also have couriers coming with more explosives. We need you to make the arrangements with our other team to have it driven from the Port of New York to Los Angeles."

"What's your target?"

"It's those kinds of questions that didn't help your employer's case."

"Understood."

"Problem with that is that we don't know where this prick is and we still don't know who the hell this woman is," Graham said.

Jansen and Dormer had presented the recording to Graham and they were in a meeting with him in the conference room.

"How's the voice recognition going?"

"Slowly," Jansen said. "We have Warren Ragucci on record, but it's going be hard to find a match on this woman. She wasn't on the NCTC list, or on any watch-list from MI-5, but initial tests have proven that the recording is genuine."

"That's good work, you two. Very good."

"I still don't understand why they would ship it to New York, just to drive it to California," Jansen said. "If they took the bomb from Virginia, then moving it to New York just to drive it to LA would be elaborate and dangerous."

"But we would chase our tails here while they attack the real target in the real city," Graham replied. "It doesn't make a difference now. I want an APB out on Ragucci, but I doubt we'll find him. He's probably long gone."

"There is still the matter of the Duckford Winery," Jansen said. "Somebody is still probably running the show from the other side of the coast."

"Hamlin's been in touch with Cochrane, and Vegas is launching a full investigation."

"What happens now?" Dormer asked.

"We'll remain watchful, but the case itself is getting kicked to our offices in Los Angeles. I'd hate to let go of it, but it's their problem now. You ought to feel good, kids, it's finally over."

On his lunch break, Dormer carried the Christmas gifts he and Eileen kept in the car into the house while the kids were at school and hid them under the bed.

"Eileen," he called. "Eileen? You home?"

He heard Eileen come out of the bathroom and met her outside. She was wearing a robe and her hair was still wet.

"You're home early," she said, somewhat surprised.

"I told you I was coming home during my lunch break."

"That's right."

"I brought the presents in and put them under the bed."

"Great job."

"Why is the shower still running?"

Before she could wrap her smirking lips into a reply, a voice came from the bathroom: "Somebody out there with you, babe?" then with a banal joke befitting a horny teenager, "A friend, maybe?"

Dormer's face dropped, and he stared at Eileen darkly.

"No, just her husband," he replied faux-casual.

166

The faucets turned off — "Oh shit" — followed by a rustling of clothes on the other side of the door.

When he wouldn't take his betrayed and angry gaze from her, Eileen said, "Are you honestly that surprised, Jim? I mean, come on."

"Where are the girls?"

"Why do you care?"

"I just don't want them to come home and see this — their mother being a whore."

"Oh, Mr. Moral High Ground, aren't you such a fucking saint. They're at your mother's, you fucking moron."

The third party stepped out of the bathroom, disheveled and pale-faced. "I didn't, know, uh," he turned to Dormer. "I didn't know she was married. I'm so—"

"Cut the shit, Conner. We met at Eileen's high-school reunion last year. We talked about foreign policy and stereo equipment. How's your wife by the way?"

"You remember that, but God forbid you remember anything having to do with our daughters," Eileen interjected.

"Shut the fuck up, Eileen."

"Hey, you can't—" Conner yelled.

Without thinking first, just on reflex, Dormer struck him once, fast. There was a crack and blood poured down his mouth and chin.

"Ahh! You prick!" he howled, stricken.

"Oh, yeah! What a big man. What a big fucking man you are!"

"I think it's fucking broken!" Conner cried.

Dormer felt shamed before Eileen said, "Don't touch it. Let it bleed for a few minutes. Go in the kitchen and put ice on it."

Conner walked to the kitchen, glaring at Eileen. Dormer turned his attention back to his wife. "One question: Why?"

"You made me."

"Oh yeah. Now I remember. I put a gun to your head and told you that if you didn't fuck that yuppie scumbag former classmate of yours I would blow your brains out."

"You don't give a fuck about me, that's why. Because you don't give a fuck about our daughters — who hate you, I'll add — because you're never home. When you are home, you're tired and you go to sleep. Your priority is that goddamn job. You love it more than us."

"I work long hours so I can keep our daughters in good schools and keep us living in a good neighborhood. Everything I do I do for our daughters and for you."

"It still doesn't make up for it, Jim. They don't care about money and schools. The quality time is what they want. I don't think I can remember the last time they saw you outside of that men's warehouse disaster you call your work clothes."

"It's called sacrifice. You ought to look it up one day during when you're not watching Oprah."

"I hate you, Jim. I hate you for making me do this — for letting this happen. You ruined this family and you ruined our marriage and I hate you for it. So... fuck... you!"

Dormer nodded and snorted. "You haven't in years."

"And if you even think about divorce, I'll just let the judge know how often you're home and I'm sure he'll side with me. So don't even fucking think about it."

"Look at the time; I have to get back to the office," he said, heavy on the sarcasm. He took pride in seeing her face contort in anger when he said it.

Dormer walked to the door and opened it. He stopped and turned back, "She's your problem now, buddy-boy. And just so you know from now: she uses too much *teeth*."

Above Grand Central Terminal is a small, dimly lit restaurant called Tropica, which often hosts corporate lawyers, stock brokers, and others with money to spend. Its close proximity to Grand Central gives it a great traffic from comers and goers. Most people that frequent Tropica wear some sort of formal attire.

Jansen went to Tropica directly from work, dressed in a dark green blouse, black dress pants and blazer. Besson was wearing dark jeans, the requisite button-down, and a royal blue button-down coat that came down past his hips to his thighs.

Besson noticed the turned heads as Jansen passed others booths, the men eventually meeting Besson's gaze. He flashed a shit-eating grin.

"I almost didn't recognize you without the leather," she joked when she made it to the table.

Besson held her face and pulled her for a kiss. She smelled of jasmine.

"I think it was time for a change."

"It looks good on you."

Tropica was lively, with people drinking some amounts of wine from large glasses, and brokers that wouldn't drink anything on tap.

"How did you find this place?" Besson asked, once they sat down.

"We were doing security sweeps at Grand Central during Thanksgiving, and I passed by on my way out one day."

"It's good to see where your focus was."

Jansen smiled. "Always."

"You seem to be in a good mood."

"I am. The case we've been working on was finally closed."

"That's great."

"You seem to be pretty happy yourself."

"As a matter of fact, I am. That conversation we had on the phone a few nights ago did me some good."

"Oh?"

A late-night phone call found him confessing to her about Sarah, Carl, and the regrets he had. Besson had learned from her that while the past cannot be changed, the future can be mitigated.

"Yeah."

"I wasn't sure if I should bring it up. I know it must be painful for you. Carl and everything else."

"It was not the best few days."

"I wish I had been there to help you. Or at least been near my phone more."

"It's fine, believe me. I didn't really want to talk. I was just so… caught up in everything. It was all happening at once; but you were there when I needed you."

Besson held her hand, and they both wanted to tell the other something they knew they shouldn't. The waitress arrived, and they ordered their drinks and dinner; *So This is Christmas* played on the radio.

"I forgot Christmas is coming," Jansen said.

"I did some shopping today, actually."

"Really. For whom?" she asked coyly.

"Myself mostly," he replied in the same tone.

"I'll have to get you something."

"No, no. You got me something for my birthday."

"Well, that was your birthday, and now it's Christmas, stupid."

"They're too close together, so don't worry about it. Let me get you something."

"We both know how this ends up, Will. I agree with you so you shut up and then I go do it anyway. You pretend you're upset when you find out, you love the gift and then we fuck."

Besson laughed heartily. "But the process is still fun, you have to give me that."

"Maybe."

"And where'd you learn that kind of language?"

"From your reaction during the *Soprano's* finale."

"You know, I almost bought a Blue Comet train set because of those last two episodes."

They laughed together.

"It's funny that you mentioned Christmas and all," Besson said.

"How so?"

"I want you to come with me to the Poconos for Christmas."

"You have a place in the Poconos?"

"No, but I rented a cabin for us from the twenty-third until January third."

"That sounds great, Will, but I don't know if I could—"

"Please, Andrea."

Besson's voice rang with an importance to his plea, and she softened.

"I'll ask for the time off."

Dr. Moira Grey returned to her table at Hubert's, where she was having dinner with Peter Lavalle and Marcus Gardner.

"I think Besson was impressed with the work we've been doing," Gardner said.

"Speaking of, is everything in place?"

"Yes, Peter. Marcus and I planted the conversation I had with Ragucci. If the authorities have discovered it by now, they'll think that Los Angeles is the new target."

"*If* is the keyword there."

"Don't worry about the recording. It was hidden well but not too difficult to find."

"*Très bon*," Lavalle with a sigh. "I think I'll go someplace warm for the rest of winter."

30

The conference room in the FBI office was active as it was usually at around this time — the morning briefing.

Jansen was sipping the coffee Dormer had given her, and noticed that David Graham's face — that always had a look of frustration and wariness — more recently wore an expression of measured calm. The reason was beginning to become apparent but nobody brought it up. Graham was a decorated agent, and had been given his position as the requisite promotion after getting shrapnel in his hip from a pipe bomb a few years back. He was well-liked and respected in the FBI. You don't fight an AD.

Secrecy tends to dominate the personal and professional lives of agents that receive the majority of their orders in manila envelopes flagged SECRET COMPARTMENTALIZED INFORMATION. This secret was different only in the way that Graham's personal life had become mixed in with his professional life. It had to remain a secret both in spite of this fact and because of it.

"Local PD picked up someone matching the description of Warren Ragucci, but it was just some poor bastard whose feathers got ruffled by a room full of half-wits. But lo and behold, late last night an off-duty pilot at LaGuardia finds the cocksucker in a pile of shallow reeds with two bullets in his head.

"Seems like the new cell that's heading to California used Ragucci the way they used Vernon Gibson. However, whether he was their courier or not, one of Gibson's trucks is missing and hasn't been found yet. Whoever's in charge wants to make sure that the trail ended with Ragucci."

"What does that mean for us? Are we back on the case?" Jansen asked.

"Our orders, as handed down from Kersh himself, are telling us to look for the truck and only the truck. Since the threat is now aimed at LA and not New York anymore, we are to simply cover our bases and make sure the truck isn't in the state anymore. Once we confirm this, the case gets handed over to the state and federal authorities between here and Cali. Kersh is giving us till the end of the week, so let's put this thing to rest.

"I want all of our information on Anderson and his associates over the last two years sent to our offices in Los Angeles, and I want our people to look it over too. Maybe we could juice this thing one last time."

"I'll see to it," Tess said.

"Also, there is the matter of the holidays coming up," Graham said. "Internet chatter has been up, but it's at the same level it usually is for this time of year. We're being cautious, but right now it doesn't look like we have too much to worry about."

"I would like to take some time off for the holidays, then," Jansen announced.

"How long?"

"The twenty-third and on. I'll back to work for the fourth."

"Jim already has off — he has first pick because he has a family."

Dormer nodded absently.

"We have enough tactical agents now, when Kersh reassigned them here for the Manhattan Bridge operation. It shouldn't be a big problem," Jansen said.

Graham sighed. "Granted, then. But I want an updated roster on my desk by closing time this evening."

"Yes, sir."

A deeper sigh. "It's gonna be an empty house this Christmas."

Personal and professional lives are never supposed to become interwoven. Allowing such a mix to occur was David Graham's first mistake, a mistake Jansen had unintentionally made as well, one whose denouement could be fatal.

There were only three people who would call Besson on his cell phone at this point. One was Andrea Jansen, the others were Martin Strughold and Peter Lavalle. Besson knew this, and when his cell phone rang, what he saw when he looked at the non-disclosed ID did not surprise him — the latter of the three possibilities.

"Hello, Will."

"Peter."

"How is everything?"

"Just fine."

"Marcus said the installation went off without any problems."

"Yeah, you put together a good crew." Besson paused. "But that's not the reason you called."

"That's right. It's getting late in the game. It'll be Christmas Eve soon, and I wanted to make sure everything is in place."

"Everything is fine on my end. When this is over, you'll send the rest of my money to the offshore account I set up?"

"I have the address and everything."

"Good."

"Do you need an out?"

"I have one set up already."

"Are you sure? I could have Moira—"

"I'm okay, really. I've had this out planned for a while. It's secure."

"What time is the bomb set to detonate?"

Besson noted the change of subject, as well as Lavalle's change of tone, as to abscond any hope of having his latent intention revealed prematurely. Lavalle probably realized Besson had — or would — become wise to this sudden initiative, and changed to a different subject that was equally as pertinent. "Night."

"Why at night? It would be better during the day, more traffic."

"At night everyone will see it — everyone will see it when it happens."

"How very operatic."

"You must've rubbed off on me," Besson replied indignantly.

Lavalle digressed after a moment. "I'll have the money sent once the reports come out."

"Yeah."

In a lengthy moment of silence, the gravity of the coming state of affairs struck both conspirators.

"I suppose this is it," Lavalle said with finality.

"Yeah."

"Good luck to you, Will."

"Thanks."

After they hung up, in the moment that Lavalle could've possibly been designing a setup to his betrayal, Besson remembered that he had — at one time — fought diligently against and abhorred men like Peter Lavalle.

Downtown, not far from ground zero, was the conventionally sized New York City office of Halifax. The guard at the front desk only nodded and smiled to Besson as he moved to the elevator.

"My dear Will," Strughold greeted as Besson entered his office. "How are you?"

"Usual, Martin."

They shook hands.

"Please sit," he offered with a hand. "What's on your mind?"

Besson looked at his watch, "Well, in case you haven't noticed, we're coming up on the deadline." He paused. "Poor choice of word. But you catch my drift."

"Indeed. I imagine you and... well that you two would be leaving soon."

"Andrea. Yeah, day after tomorrow."

"Saying goodbye tomorrow, then? To the city?"

"Yeah. I plan on riding this out far from here."

"I don't blame you, but if you did stick around it would give you a wonderful tan I'm sure."

Besson gave him a half-hearted smile. Strughold eyed the bar at the corner of the room.

"What the hell, it's after noon."

A stoli and a JD. A clink, a drink, and two empty glasses.

"I talked to Peter earlier today. I think he's planning on killing me."

Strughold nodded. "I'm not at all surprised. That better-safe-than-sorry stuff."

"I think I should..."

"I'll take care of it."

"Are you sure?"

Strughold winked. "Maybe the Sons of Liberty find out Peter screwed their boss over. I think they'd be upset to hear that, don't you?"

"Thank you, Martin… for everything."

There was a long pause. Their comfortable smiles gave to a sincere understanding of what happens next.

"I suppose this is it, then," Strughold said. They shook hands. "It was good working with you. I'm proud of you, my boy. This is a difficult situation, and what you're doing — the decision you've made, the acts you've had to commit, the things you'll have to live with — it's probably the hardest thing anyone in history has ever had to do, to live with."

"I never thought it'd be easy. I'd hate to think what kind of person I'd be if I found it easy. But I don't have any delusions about any of this. I think I'll be ready for Hell when I get there," Besson said.

"We'll let's not reserve you table there just yet. I'll see you again soon."

"We'll speak after… *after*."

"I should hope so."

31

This was the last day — bright and clear and so resolutely ordinary. It was for that reason that Besson woke early, a rush of panic searing through him in the first light of day. Andrea, curled up in the blankets beside him, stirred peacefully, a pleasant dream occupying her. This was their last day home before leaving, as many others would, only to find there wouldn't be a home to return to.

It was because this day began so quietly and innocuously that Besson couldn't help but expect the other shoe to drop. Experience had taught him to expect the worst, but the day itself was unsuspecting. It was the same experience which translated to a twelve-year career in the Bureau that not only made him think this way but also made him only take facts into account. And by all accounts everything was fine. Somehow it was this same teaching that escaped him now. Worry and general anxiety overrode any and all logic and evidence contrary to his belief that there was no hidden danger, no silent phantasm awaiting a lapse in diligence. With a deep breath and a clearing of his thoughts, he reminded himself that these fears were unwarranted and unfounded and went about this final day as normal as it promised. And, if anything, to at least say goodbye.

Andrea woke and left for work, a slight smirk of anticipation on her face. She knew it was their last day too, though she was excited for reasons both dissimilar to and the same as Besson's. After she left he began his long and final farewell to the city of lights. He walked the streets and avenues, window shopped and languidly browsed, strolled and toured as if he were some out-of-towner going on a sight-seeing tour of Manhattan during the holidays. His lunch came from a Grey's Papaya, he snacked from street vendors.

By the most expensive jewelry stores along Fifth Avenue he huddled among the masses of last minute shoppers and purchased the gift for Andrea that he had ordered and had engraved. It was separate from the letter he had written for her, a sort of contingency if things went awry — sometimes cooler heads couldn't match an embattled heart. In its entirety he came to realize the depth of his care for her and the irony in his unrevealed role in her life: a dichotomous role of both protector and endangerer.

He would take to this role one last time, placing her in the implacable harm of being in his presence, only to deliver her to the last refuge, safe and away from even the sight of a burning sky, or the silent scream of a bomb detonating — a city writing a final tragic and bloody chapter in its short history. It would also be from that distance that Besson would close the curtain on the opera, and in doing so, do the same on an era.

As the sun began its descent, and the azure sky was slowly overtaken by the blue-black drapes of night, Besson reflected on this day that began in panic, in fear of its possible, underlying malignance, to find a day beyond reproach — a day, Besson considered, Lou Reed could only have written about. However, he knew when to quit while he was ahead and decided to wait for her at her apartment, instead of picking her up at work. He would surprise her with flowers and dinner, they would make love and he would surrender himself to her, to the warmth of her hearth, to the promise she represented, to the life she meant to him.

32

Friday, December 23rd

"So how did you score this place in the Pocono's?" Jansen asked.

Besson was driving, Jansen next to him in his Altima, well on their way to their rented home in the Pocono's. It was the last refuge, a place far away from the epicenter and fallout; a small slice of untouched land, nestled far from the bitter city that was about to become nothing more than Scorched Earth.

"Kickback from the mob. I used to ignore the missing trucks of cigarettes and Johnnie Walker blue and they owed me a favor."

"Well thank God it wasn't from anything illegal."

They smirked at each other knowingly. Besson took his right hand off the wheel and placed it on hers.

Jansen had noticed his acts of affection recently, just subtle nuances that came off as tender and endearing, which was a side to Besson that she embraced wholly. Their lovemaking as well had changed over the last few weeks. It was passionate, even more so than before. He also seemed less tentative, and appeared to brood less since their conversation shortly after Carl McDowell's funeral.

When they stopped at a gas station, Jansen decided to walk around for a minute and stretch her legs. Once she was safely out of range, Besson stopped pumping the gas and walked around to the passenger side of the car where her cell phone was on the dashboard. It had no reception. Besson was relieved. He checked the PDA in his jacket, the electronic digits counting down until the detonation. It seemed to be running fine. The news on the radio mentioned nothing was awry; there were no alerts and no rumors mentioned on the news. Granted, it was possible that the press was not aware of something that the government was — it happened frequently — but Besson took this as a good omen. He looked up to the sky above him for a long moment, and back down to the PDA. He stuffed it in his jacket and walked back to the other side of the car.

In thirty-six hours it would all be over, and yet just beginning.

33

The drizzle was getting heavier, and David Graham popped the collar on his brown trench coat accordingly. The slick sidewalks and streets slowed his already sluggish pace, but he never slipped or fell. All these years relying on his cane made him an expert in using it. He could be quite nimble, but obviously still unable to work in the field. He missed needing only two legs to get around, and he missed being young. He blinked angrily as the drizzle hit his face with greater range. He popped two Valium while waiting for a light to change.

Tess called Dormer over to her station. She had just gotten off the phone and looked vexed. She punched something up on her computer.

"What is it?"

"I just got off the phone with Homeland Security."

"And?"

"They just got through going over the Port of New York. They found traces of radiation. There was also a warehouse a quarter of a mile from the place with other radioactive materials with the same consistency as a nuclear weapon."

"Christ. But didn't the President ask us to do that last month?"

"It was kicked to Homeland."

"Christ. What type of bomb are we dealing with?"

"Hydrogen bomb. The radiation at the warehouse and the port match."

"They probably had the bomb shipped here and then worked on it at the warehouse."

"It gets worse. Remember a few months ago when that convoy was attacked and DC sent out a report that one of their nuclear weapons had been stolen by some sort of terrorist consortium?" Tess turned her attention to her computer screen and pointed. "Take a look at their report. It was a hydrogen bomb that was stolen."

"Do you have any idea of what method of delivery they could use?"

"Judging from the container it came in from Duckford Winery, it could be a suitcase bomb, or something that could be later attached to a missile or dropped from the air."

"Jesus Christ. Alright, I'm gonna try to get Bill Hamlin on the line. Call Graham, and tell them what you told me."

"What about Vegas?"

"We shouldn't make that call until we're sure if it's a match. Try to get the schematics of it from their database, and any other kind of information that could identify it. On second thought, I think I'll call them. It sounds like it *is* a secondary attack from the Sons of Liberty and they should be dealt with. I'll call LA too."

"Right."

The cabin that Besson had rented appeared old-fashioned from the outside. It was of wooden construction and had the look of historic elegance to it. On the inside it was lavish with dark rugs, a heating system, a large bedroom, a Jacuzzi, and a full bathroom. There was also a fully decorated Christmas tree next to a fire place.

Besson had Jansen close her eyes before he opened the door.

"My God, Will. It's beautiful," she said.

"Are you glad you came?"

"Yeah. It's amazing here."

They unpacked and settled in. Jansen and Besson looked around. They had brought up food and bottles champagne with them, and drank one in the Jacuzzi.

"So when do I get to see my presents?"

"At Christmas."

Jansen smiled. "Hard ass."

"I thought you liked that quality of mine." He smiled.

"I think I need another look." She took off the top of her bikini, did the same to her bottoms. Besson followed suit.

After a long duration there, he sat back, with Jansen with her back on his abdomen, both wrapped in the bubbling water, still naked, holding each other.

"It's a shame we'll have to go back to reality after Christmas," Jansen said. "I love it here."

Besson was silent for a long moment. "Yeah. It's a shame."

Graham passed through the doors of the office sluggishly, his eyes half-closed. The noise contained in its borders seemed only to be in the background, which was also spinning.

Tess came up to him and briefed him on some sort of situation involving Welles Cochrane, or a bomb. Or both. It was something, assuredly. His instincts took over for a moment and he told her to get Bill Hamlin down to the office.

He knew something was wrong. He felt he was moving himself from outside his body. His head felt constricted, as did his chest.

He made his way to his office and closed the door. He went to his mini-fridge and pulled out a bottled water after two tries. After a call Graham left his office again. He still had his rain-spattered trench coat on.

"Are you going out again, David?" Walker asked. "We could really use your help on this hydrogen bomb threat."

"I'm just going to the bathroom," he replied.

Once there, Graham placed his cane over by the sink and threw cold water on his face. Becoming dizzy in that bent position, Graham moved for his cane but failed and fell backward, down onto the floor. His hip was on fire, as was his lower back now. The constricting in his chest made things go black, as the entire world continued to spin.

34

Saturday, December 24th

The area surrounding the cabin in the Poconos was mostly forest. The trees had no leaves on their branches and there were no longer many leaves on the ground. It had snowed recently, and not all of it melted.

Andrea Jansen walked around this area in passivity, enjoying the brisk air that seemed to taste differently than in the city. It was better here, she decided. It had been a rather warm winter, albeit some rough patches of weather and a cold front here and there. Now, both in the city and in the Poconos, the weather had become crisp, and refreshing, but not too cold. It was good football weather. The early morning sun glistened off the dew and the mostly melted snow and seemed to glow. The tiny spots of light seemed to dance in the reflection. The entire area, in its natural beauty, almost seemed to be alive and untouched by the aggressive and steadfast industrialization of land by humanity. This was their little slice of heaven, as Besson had promised it would be.

Besson had woken up shortly after Jansen left, as his PDA had gone off, signaling the necessity to punch in the code at the twelve-hour mark. He did, and tried to go back to sleep, but couldn't rest his mind, which chattered away with flurried thoughts about tomorrow's world. He turned on the television in the bedroom. Both CNN and Fox News Channel had nothing of interest, and Besson dozed on and off for another hour. His half-awake, half-asleep dreams were frenzied ones, full of bright lights and bitter endings. There were things in these diluted considerations that were horrible enough to wake him up totally, nude and in a cold sweat. He dared not tell Jansen what he had seen in those dreams, and he tried not to remember them.

They ate lunch together quietly and discussed their surroundings. They had champagne with lunch, which Jansen mixed in with a glass of orange juice. The lunch itself was bountiful and Jansen was surprised by his culinary ability. Afterwards, they walked along the area together, hand in hand, and would kiss each other tenderly. Never had Besson felt as content. He was not pensive. He again imagined that life he had so fleetingly considered with Andrea Jansen — a small wedding, a house in a docile and sleepy suburb, holiday dinners, anniversaries spent sipping wine by the fireplace, a white picket fence, a dog, Fourth of July barbeques, first days of school, watching the kids open gifts on early Christmas mornings, birthday parties, little league games, parent-teacher conferences, sunsets, grandkids, a fitting death from old age surrounded by loved ones, snowy winters and warm summers, a slower paced life.

Now, it seemed plausible, something just within reach. This pleased him, and so did she. It was soothing. The way he had always wanted his life to be.

Once they returned, Besson excused himself so he could shower and Jansen went into the bedroom and watched television.

Besson felt the hot water on his body and his muscles relaxed. He was not tired, but was ready to fall asleep the longer he remained there. It was sweet rapture.

Finally, the hull of secrets that kept the outside world away from them breached. Besson didn't hear it at first, but Jansen did. An alarm. Besson soon heard it and heard her footsteps moving to the kitchen where his jacket hung on the chair at the kitchen table. He called to her, telling her to stop, but she didn't hear him.

He was already dressing when the alarm went off. He went to the medicine cabinet where there was a moist cloth, doused in chloroform in a small plastic box. (He had taken the precaution of making this cloth when he first booked the cabin. He had taken an earlier drive there, bringing food, the Christmas tree, turning on the heat). He stuffed the cloth in the back pocket of his pants and ran into the kitchen.

Jansen pulled the PDA out Besson's jacket and read: SECOND COM-
MAND CODE REQUIRED. COUNTDOWN SURCEASED.

Once the detonation is paused, and the code was punched in to restart
it, the countdown would resume, covering the elapsed time, so the detonation would happen at the exact time it was set. It was a device of genius.

"What the hell is this, Will?" Jansen asked when he came barreling into
the kitchen. She already had a notion, and the tears in her eyes reflected
this. "What the hell is this?"

She knew.

"Andrea, please—"

"What the fuck, Will?"

"It's a remote detonator," he said, defeated.

Besson revealed to her the story of his time away from the Bureau
— his alliance and collaboration with a non-specific terrorist syndicate, his
idea of stealing a nuclear weapon, with the target being Manhattan. It all
came undone, and Besson spoke in a cold monotone that Jansen had never
heard before.

When he was finished, she was in tears, and was barely about to choke
out: "So this was a lie? *Us?*" She then realized just how much of their relationship had relied on equivocation.

"No, of course not. I cared for you then and now. That's why you're
here."

"I don't believe you."

"Think about it. When did I ever talk shop with you? Never. Because I
didn't want to; I wasn't with you for *that.*"

"Why are you doing this?"

"Because it has to be done, Andrea," he replied. "After September 11th
we were progressing as human beings — we were stronger, we were kind,
we understood the miracle of life, the will to survive. We could have created a lasting betterment in society, and we could've become a center of
change in America. A new way to look at things, a refined view. But the
attack didn't last long in people's memories. Soon enough, we all started
back toward that immeasurable apathy and mistrust.

"We didn't have enough time to make sense of what happened, we didn't have enough time to understand it, or to heal from it. Instead we let the need for revenge take over — and look where it's gotten us. Things need to change — change back to the way it was just after this happened.

"In order to show people how special we are — how lucky we are to be alive — we have to take those lives from them, and put a mirror to their faces and show them who they really are. The only way to make people appreciate their lives is to take some away. Enough to make them never forget how lucky we are as survivors. It's the only way to achieve a lasting peace."

"If all of these people are supposed to die, why am I here with you?"

"I don't want you to die. I know you — you're a caring and kind person who hasn't been corrupted by these times. You're innocent and you don't deserve what's coming."

"You can't force things — even peace — onto people, Will. We have to learn from their own mistakes, through their own lives. We're all like that, and we won't learn any other way."

"Then we need a new teacher," he muttered with a cruelty she had never seen.

"What about the millions of people back in Manhattan?"

"Ingrates, mostly."

"What about the portion of people that aren't?" Her voice was cracking. "What about *them*, Will?! Huh? What about them?"

"Sometimes innocent lives are taken for the greater good. That's the way things work."

"You're a monster," she said, her voice filled with revulsion. "A murderer."

"NO!" Besson boomed. "I am a patriot! A humanist! I love this country — and I love that city — but times have changed and we have to change with them."

After a glowering stillness, "You believe this, don't you? You really do." Jansen's voice emphasized the fact that her mind had just begun to process this epiphany.

"Yes."

She wept for several seconds, her head down. When Besson moved closer to her, she looked back up. Her mascara had been botched with tears, and it was running down her face.

"Where is the bomb?" she demanded; her voice resolute in its reverberation. She was strong again.

"I can't tell you."

"Fine."

Jansen smashed the PDA along the counter, and Besson ran towards her; though he dared not strike her. She hit him hard in the chest, and he fell back against the kitchen table.

"Why did you do that?"

"Because I love this country, too." Her voice was cracking again.

Besson was motionless, processing these events, and thinking of a positive outcome. There was only one option left. He swallowed hard and sighed.

Jansen moved closer to him.

"I have to take you in," she said, but she didn't move. She couldn't. Not against *him*.

In one fluid motion, Besson lunged at her, the swabbed pad on his right palm, his left arm hooking around her neck. He placed the pad over her mouth, and held her just tightly enough to keep her from escaping.

As he pressed the cloth on her mouth, he whispered in her ear, "You may not realize this now — or ever — but I did this in all our best interests, and I kept you here because I love you too much to let what must happen to me now happen to you."

Besson carried her and laid her out on the bed. He destroyed both of their cell phones and sat at the kitchen table alone for quite a while — an hour at least — and quietly processed what he must now do. This wasn't such a foreign concept to him. He knew the risks going in, and he was ready to deal with the realization that he was about to die.

He wept for only a few minutes. At first for himself, and then for the life he had to give up — the life he had become comfortable in; the one he would have to leave behind.

Once at his car, he took his SIG-Sauer from the trunk and attached it in its holster to his hip and pocketed his old FBI ID. He didn't notice the gifts he purchased for Jansen were still in the backseat of his Altima.

He got in and started the engine. He paused again, staring out into the sleepy and deserted forest area. McDowell's funeral flashed in his mind, specifically the engraving on his tombstone:

"Dulce Et Decorum Est," *sweet and fitting it is to die for one's country.*

Besson agreed, and counted how many operas he knew that ended tragically.

35

Besson's restraint and unwillingness to do harm to Andrea Jansen caused her current situation. She was awake, though barely. He hadn't held the chloroform-soaked rag tight enough or long enough over her mouth. It also didn't help that the rag had dried up since his original application some days ago. She awoke to the world spiraling and distorted. The walls were diluted and blurred, seeming to move in wave like fashion. Disoriented, as if suffering from vertigo, Jansen was unaware of her surroundings or what had led her to this point. Her arms and legs seemed heavy and she felt as if she had moved them several times, but hadn't in actuality. In a last, desperate struggle, she tensed her body enough and with all she could gather, she rolled off the bed, and fell hard onto the floor. She succumbed again to the emptiness for several seconds.

When she awoke again, her resolve was strengthened. The blow to her body from the fall cleared her mind substantially. She was able to move with a greater ease, though not much. It was unclear as to what had happened still but she was able to clear her mind long enough to move again. At this point she could only crawl, and she did, to the sink. It took the strength she had in both of her arms to pull her up, and she leaned her weight over the sink to keep from falling over. She cupped her hands and drank from the faucet.

She thought she was going to throw up, but only dry heaved a few times. Time passed swirled around her just as the walls had, and she had no concept of how much time had passed. In reality, there was a duration of eight minutes from the time she woke up until she reached the sink. She drank more and kept her eyes open, trying not to fall under again. In about a half hour she was able to stand on her own again. The color returned to her face and body and walking was no longer a detrimental enterprise.

Her mind was clear and she realized what had brought her to this moment. She immediately ran for her cell phone, which she noticed was in pieces on the table and floor. So was his. The cabin had no phone either. The car was gone. She checked her purse. She had, as always, her ID, her badge and her service weapon.

Jansen went over the lay of the land in her mind. If she followed the mainland down a mile, she'd reach the road again. There was a gas station five miles down that road. If she could catch a ride, she'd hike there and use a pay phone. She needed to call the office, warn them of the nuclear threat… *the bomb could go off anytime*, she thought to herself. She cursed herself for not thinking to check the television, recognizing the fact she could already be too late.

Jansen began her walk, her jacket wrapped tightly around her. She went over the plan in her mind a thousand times, just to get her mind off the fact that she was sending Besson, the only man she ever — dare she say it? — *loved*, to a lifetime prison sentence, or, in the more probable resolution, his bereavement.

36

Stringent safety measures had gotten him this far. He was always alert and lived on fact and instinct; a talent that had taken years to properly develop and accrue. Turning his radio on to the local news channel was the least he could do at this point. His cell phone had no reception and therefore no means of contacting anyway who would be his eyes and ears in New York. The local news, though often interrupted by static, would have to be sufficient for the time being.

A newscaster cut through Besson's list of safety measures to adhere to when he returned to the city: "…Mr. Strughold making the announcement earlier today…"

"It is with great pleasure that I announce today that we at Halifax are in the final stages of negotiations with the United States military. We have been actively pursuing this contract for some time now and at last we believe that we are nearing the end of a very long process, expecting to reach a mutually beneficial arrangement.

"Over the course of our provisional five-year contract we will be exploring new technologies for use in the military with a focus on heavy weapons and armaments so we can better protect our boys and help deflect the attacks of our nation's enemies so we may better ensure victory on the battlefield with less casualties on our side of the fence…"

The reporter: "Although Mr. Strughold's words are not without a patriotic overtone, he skirted questions of how much the contract is worth to his organization, though rumors have been circulating at an estimated 4.5 billion."

Strughold's statement continued, answering a question, *"Yes, some of the tech we'll be developing will be focused on satellite imagery of missiles and targets so as to assist our boys behind the computers with real-time feeds…"*

Further confessions:

"…while I wouldn't say that this is a wartime economy I wouldn't say that it isn't either…

"…strictly military technology…"

The truth came through like a red hot bullet. Besson realized then he had been blinded, blame for it being shared by Strughold and himself.

Shaken to the marrow, Besson stopped his car on the side of the empty road. He breathed and discovered another truth: the opera was still going on, though the choreographer was changing the moves without telling the director. The players, the orchestra and the stage had already been set, and now as the final act was reaching its climax, as Besson had previously, Strughold was writing and altering the future as he saw fit. Besson, who had come to master that ability himself, saw fit to make changes that would set it right.

Reaching for his SIG and sliding the clip home, Besson decided that the final act was to take a new direction. The curtain lifted.

37

Miles behind Besson, Greg Burke was driving his Ford down the same barren road, and making great time. The snow had melted from the road, and had moved off to the side; not that there was much snow to begin with. This winter had been rather tame.

He was humming along to the song on the radio — *Dead Flowers* — when he saw a figure ahead. The figure, of medium height, was walking off to the side of the road, and turned as Burke approached in his Ford. He thought about slowing down, even stopping to see what this person was doing in the middle of nowhere — perhaps go as far as offer a ride—but a troubling superstition he remembered made him rebuke that idea. He decided to keep going and not even look at the figure when he passed.

The figure had a different idea, and shifted itself into the middle of the road, right in Burke's path.

Do the crazies ever stop?

He swerved to avoid, but the figure — which he now recognized to be a woman — again blocked his new course and pulled something from her back. Burke felt his heart drop as he slammed the breaks, realizing that this wandering woman was pointing a gun at him. She shouted something before she started to move closer to his car, which didn't register. The only thing that registered in his mind was that he was afraid.

The woman moved into the backseat of the car, the gun still trained staunchly at him. Her nose and her cheeks were rosy, but her forehead was moist with perspiration. She had been walking for quite a while it seemed, and her body heat was combating the chill of the outside. She pulled something from her back again, with her free hand. Burke flinched, but when he looked back he saw a federal ID. This wanderer was a federal agent, or so the ID had him believe, he thought.

"My name is Andrea Jansen," she said. "I'm an agent with the Federal Bureau of Investigation." She decided to be kind, but scare him enough so he would think better of trying to be a hero. "I'm on assignment and I need some help. Is that your phone there, on the dash?"

Burke's throat was rough and dry. After an attempt he choked.

"Okay then..."

Jansen moved over and was now directly behind him. She jammed the gun into the back of his head; an act she felt was wrong. "I want you to slowly take your right hand and reach for the phone, and slowly drop it into the back seat next to me." Jansen watched him intently, and noticed how his hand shook. He dropped the phone next to her as requested.

No reception.

"Son of a bitch." She put her gun away. "Turn around to me."

Burke did slowly, but his eyes were closed. "Look, I didn't get a good look at your face, I can give you whatever you want. The car, my wallet, my phone — whatever. Please just don't kill me," he begged, starting to weep.

Jansen sighed, her patience was running thin.

"I told you, I'm a federal agent. I'm not going to kill you. There's a gas station going in your direction about five miles down. Do you know it?"

"Yeah."

"Drive me there now, and you'll be on your way again in no time."

Burke did as requested. The drive seemed to take forever, even though he was speeding. Jansen noticed something gleam on his hand in the sunlight.

"Married?"

"What? Oh. Yeah. Two years."

"I'm sorry for having to do this to you."

Burke nodded.

"You'll be back to her in no time," she promised.

Burke was too scared to ask any follow up questions, or notice the discrepancy of what she was claiming. He just drove.

38

Strughold loved to watch himself on television. He never thought he would ever be on television, even after Halifax became a household name for its many controversial moves, and when it became apparent he would have to defend himself at press conferences, he felt a spark of fear at the beginning. He now took a great pleasure in seeing himself on the news, as if he were a movie star. He loved the way he was over with the press now, the way he was able to manipulate the people through the press — going from pariah to patriot in a matter of a few conferences. It **was** empowering.

All day today he found himself staring out at the cityscape: last good-byes. He wondered if photographers would auction off pictures of the pre-bomb New York City in the days, weeks, months, years and decades that follow. Upon thinking of his coming pay from the government, he laughed at the chump change the photographers would get in comparison.

In just a few more hours his legacy would be secured. A hero. The irony of this was never lost on him, and it made him laugh dryly to himself.

His office phone rang and interrupted his reflection.

"Martin, it's Will."

Strughold looked at his watch, felt the sting of panic. "What's wrong, you're supposed to be gone already."

"There was a wrinkle. I'm heading back into the city now."

"Jesus Christ — what the fuck happened?"

"The remote is gone."

Full on panic. "What do you mean gone? Are we fucked? Are we *fucked*, Will?"

"I was made by the woman I've been seeing." Before Strughold could ask, Besson told him, "She's been taken out of the equation, don't worry."

"It's a little late for that. Is the remote salvageable?"

"Destroyed."

"I was wrong. We aren't fucked. This is a snuff film. What now?"

"We need to talk about another option."

"What other—"

"Not over the phone. I'm about an hour from your office."

"Alright, fine. I'll be here."

Strughold placed the receiver back on the cradle and held his hand there for a long moment. Something was wrong, he knew it. Something different in Besson's voice; under the urgency there was something burgeoning.

The TV: "...*while I wouldn't say that this is a wartime economy...*"

"Shit."

Strughold typed his login key into his desktop computer and patched into the security cameras. He watched and waited. Ready.

Besson had only actually been twenty minutes away. Strughold smiled at the game he thought he was playing — catch the man off guard, unready.

The security guard recognized him and waved him through with barely as much as a glance — son of a bitch.

As Besson left the view of the camera Strughold noticed the unbuttoning on Besson's coat, a rise on the side of his hip.

In a drawer on his desk was a lockbox. Strughold fumbled with the keys, freed the silenced 9mm inside and hid it under his suit coat at the small of his back, and made himself a drink, praying that his fears were not justified.

Once at the gas station, Burke sped away quickly, almost colliding with another car, when Jansen dialed the field office — Graham's office.

"This is Hamlin,"

"Bill?"

"Andrea, I didn't expect—"

"Listen, there's a nuclear bomb in Manhattan. It's going to be detonating soon. I'm talking hours."

"How do you know this?"

"I know the person masterminding it."

"How?"

"Look, I can't explain this over the phone. Have Tess extrapolate a list of likely targets, and get a photo of former FBI agent Will Besson. He's the suspect and he's driving a dark Nissan Altima. I don't know the plate number. He's about six foot two, auburn hair, wearing a long coat, navy blue button-down and black pants...and I need a pick-up at my location."

"Where are you?"

"I'm at a gas station in the Poconos."

"I'll have Don trace your location. I'll send Jim in a chopper to—"

"No, you come."

"Why?"

"Just do it!"

Hamlin understood the urgency in Jansen's voice. Pardoning the presumption of her speech, he was in the helicopter when it arrived to pick her up.

She climbed in and put on a headset to talk to Hamlin without having to contend with the sound of the helicopter. She closed the circuit so only the two of them could hear the conversation.

"Tell me what happened," Hamlin ordered, rather flustered.

"I was with Besson here in the Poconos. I found his PDA when some sort of alarm went off on it. It said that the detonation was paused because another code needed to be entered. When I confronted him he confessed that he planted a bomb in the city."

"Then what?"

"I smashed the PDA and he knocked me out — chloroform I think."

"Where is he now?"

"Heading back to Manhattan I imagine."

"He could be on the lam."

"I doubt it. For an operation like this, don't you think there'd be a manual trigger, in case of an event like this — if the remote detonator was destroyed?"

"Good God."

"What are you doing back here, anyway? At the field office?" she said after cumbersome silence.

"Agent Graham had an accident." His voice was taut with a grief that he had been trying to hide since its inception.

"Accident?"

"He overdosed on a mix of Tramadol and Valium. He had two prescriptions, one from Dr. Parks, the other from his private physician nobody knew about. He was using them for the pain in his hip and also as a relaxant for his anxiety."

"Is he alright?"

"Doctors induced coma. It's too early to tell just yet." Hamlin cleared his throat. "I'm going to need to know the extent of your relationship with Besson." He was obviously uncomfortable asking the question.

Jansen peered through the window, looking out on the sky, and the clouds. She then looked down at her hands, which were folded in her lap. Hamlin had never seen her like this. "We're... involved," she conceded.

Hamlin felt strange, hearing her admit this, in the present tense. He digressed and comforted her, placing his hand on hers.

"Where is Tess on that list?" she asked, after a minute.

Hamlin hesitated.

"What is it?"

"Andrea, I'm on orders from the President to remand you into custody until this matter is resolved."

"He thinks I'm involved in this?"

"He thinks you're too close to this thing to be involved — that your personal involvement in this case would make you a liability," he corrected. He paused, then, "I'm sorry."

"Bill, I need you to reinstate me on a provisional basis."

"I can't do that."

"Think about it, Bill. I know this guy, I know how he thinks. I can be an asset."

"Considering the extent of your relationship with this man, I cannot allow it."

"You know I can deal with it, and if you or President Ellison want my badge when it's over, you can have it; but right now, I'm your best chance of finding him before the bomb goes off." The strong sense of determination had returned to her voice.

Hamlin capitulated. "DHS, and NYPD are circulating photos of Besson and we have tactical teams checking airports and searching areas with a high population density. We have HRT scrambling. Traffic going in and out of the city has been terrible. If he's driving he won't be in the city for quite a while. That gives us an edge."

"How much does the public know?"

"Nothing. They think it's just a security measure right now. Ellison wants to keep this quiet for the time being. He is, however, considering instituting certain protocols."

"Martial Law?"

"Negative. Ellison doesn't want any riots to break out. However, he is considering imposing an evacuation protocol."

"Because that definitely wouldn't start a shit-storm," she muttered dryly. She noticed she had borrowed from Besson's wit, and felt her shield beginning to break. She took a deep breath and looked out the window again.

At that moment the sky never seemed so blue.

39

"Do you think this is a wise course of action, sir?" Kersh asked. He and Ronald Kurtzweil were in the Oval Office, conferencing with President Ellison. Both stood before him, grimly.

Kurtzweil was a tall, stone-faced man with broad shoulders. He had served in Vietnam as a soldier and in the Gulf War as a general. In Kersh's opinion, Kurtzweil was a pessimist by trade, though he may just be a realist. Kurtzweil had a full head of hair, dominated by grays. He had a healthy weight to him, and had the eyes of a war veteran hidden behind thin rimmed, lightly tinted glasses.

"I don't want to start a mass exodus, Al," Ellison said.

Kersh hated being called Al.

"Sir, with all due respect, this is a dangerous bet. The FBI reported that a former agent is likely in Manhattan right now, attempting to detonate a nuclear weapon. He has training, sir — he is probably very good at avoiding detection, as well as having a great deal of knowledge in our strategies. I suggest getting as many people out of the city as we can right now before it's too late. The sun is setting, and once it's dark we'll stand a next-to-nothing chance of finding him."

"Ron, you're my chief advisor, what do you say?"

"Reports from the FBI office in Manhattan claim that the bomb is hydrogen. With wind persistence, we're projecting a loss of two million at least, with blow-back hitting other boroughs. If this bomb goes off, it will be bad no matter what we decide."

"How are local and federal doing over there?"

"They're doing the best they can. Reports are rather hopeful. They think they could stop this attempt in time. DHS is heading up radiation scans right now, as well as questioning those on the NCTC list. FBI has HRT out patrolling high-risk targets with Delta Force teams. Force has also been assigned to attack the suspected Sons of Liberty compound. NSA is right now watching internet chatter as well as air traffic."

"Have NEST deployed," Ellison ordered. "Tell them this one's for real."

"Sir, there's something else," Kersh mentioned.

"What is it, Al?"

"I've granted the reinstatement of Andrea Jansen."

"You did *what?*"

"Sir, she's the best chance we have at finding Besson. She knows him better than anyone. She's a resource we need to use to full potential."

"I thought you said she was unfit, and would likely pose a liability. Frankly, I'm not certain of her loyalties."

"Bill Hamlin has given me his word that's she's fit and that she's on our side. He'll keep her on a tight leash, sir."

"Very well, but I want reports on her every fifteen minutes."

"Understood."

"What do we know about this Besson individual?"

"We know only what his records say. Capable agent for the FBI's Behavioral Analysis Unit and the CTD. At a Career Board meeting after a questionable shooting he snapped and quit. FBI Director Bowman made him the poster child of his Zero Tolerance policy," Kersh said.

"When did this happen?"

"Few years ago."

"And where did he go after that?"

"Presumably west where he was aided by the Sons of Liberty — the same group which may also be responsible for the attempt on the Manhattan Bridge — and he returned to New York sometime in the fall. He knew Agent Jansen from his days in the Bureau and met again when he returned to New York. As of now we don't know if it was serendipity or purposeful. Jansen seems to believe their relationship had nothing to do with his plans — he never took much of an interest in national security measures."

"Probably because he knew he wouldn't be found, *because* he knew how to get around them every step of the way," Ellison bellowed. "Do we have any idea who his coconspirators are?"

"We're assuming he was in some way connected to Josh Anderson. That's all we have," Kurtzweil replied.

"Sir, there is still the matter of evacuation," he reminded them.

"I am canceling it for the time being."

"At least impose martial law," Kurtzweil said in a prodding and forceful voice.

"No. Give our people time. If we don't get any results within the next two hours I will go public with this news and invoke an evacuation mandate." Ellison sighed heavily. He was drained.

Kurtzweil shot Kersh an unforgiving glare.

"How did things get *this* bad?" Ellison muttered to no one in particular. "When did our own people lose faith in us?"

"Around the time the Towers fell," Kersh said.

40

When he found himself outside of the double doors that blocked Strughold's office from the outside, he paused for breath. As he gripped the doorknob he noticed his palms weren't sweating, his hands weren't shaking. He had no fear or reservations. He felt nothing.

A quick knock on the door was the only indication he gave that he was present, and entered before Strughold could reply.

Strughold stood from his desk, turning the monitor on his computer off, and setting the vodka he was drinking on the glass coaster on the desk. He walked over to Besson, extending a hand, "Good to see you safe, Will."

Besson hesitated only for a second before taking his hand — a firm but friendly shake. "I was surprised you're still here on Christmas Eve."

"I'm catching a red-eye back home to make it in time for my family." A pause. "Sit." He gestured with a hand.

He hesitated before walking ahead, his back to Strughold, taking a seat in front of the desk. Strughold sat behind the desk, reclining in his chair on reflex, barely suppressing a grunt.

Besson's eyes narrowed for an instant.

"You look weathered. Drink?"

His mind screaming, Besson was hardly able to hear the offer over the roar that demanded he kill Strughold now. "I'm fine, thanks."

A beat. "Tell me the situation."

"My girlfriend found the remote, smashed it."

"That was very stupid of you, Will. Careless. Does the Bureau know?"

"Hard to say."

Bullshit. "What did you do to her... Andrea. Right?"

"Yeah." He felt like vomiting just lying about it. "I had to kill her."

"We'll have to put things off to ready another remote."

"I don't know if we have enough time."

"Then what do you propose we do?"

"I could detonate the bomb manually."

Strughold scoffed, though comfortable again in Besson's presence at the resurgence of his fanaticism. "Let's not get carried away — you were operating on a hunch this entire time. The timer will run out tomorrow night and the bomb will go off on schedule. We're still in the clear."

Besson rubbed his fingers over his eyes and sighed, tired.

"You've been run ragged today, haven't you?" Strughold asked.

"Yeah."

"And I *am* sorry about what you had to do to your girlfriend."

"Andrea."

"Yes. Andrea. Sorry."

Another sigh. "I think I could go for that drink now."

Strughold's lips curled into a dark smirk. "JD on the rocks?"

The same smirk. "Always."

Strughold, up slowly, Besson waiting to see his back. Strughold, half turned toward the bar, grabbed at his 9mm and drew a beat as he saw movement in his peripheral vision.

Besson was just out of his chair, coat open, hand on his holstered SIG.

"Damnit, Will," Strughold groaned. "Goddamnit."

Besson said absently, "I was right."

"Probably. But for right now I'm going to have to ask that you disarm — slowly take the gun from the holster, remove the magazine and kick it away."

Besson obliged, his eyes — burning embers of his ire staring back at Strughold — never faltering from Strughold's view.

"You can put the gun on the desk now. A long pause. "Goddamnit, Will. We were so close and you had to go and fuck it up by pulling this shit. Is the remote really destroyed?"

"Like Dillinger."

Strughold put his gun arm down. "Son of a bitch. What do you think you were going to do by coming here and blowing me away?"

"I was planning on confronting you, killing you, making the government aware of what you were doing and then detonating the bomb manually."

"Very operatic, Will. I have to say. I knew you were out there — fanatical even — but I never thought you were a self-righteous, blind, idiot."

"At least I'm not a money-driven monster. Even then, you were brilliant. The entire thing. You fed your Middle East contract cancellation to the press like candy. It turned you and Halifax from enemy sympathizers to patriots. By severing your ties with the Middle East you left the door open to do business with the government for weapons."

"It's the foundation on which this economy is based, Will. This whole thing — capitalism at its finest," Strughold said.

"You were planning on letting millions of people die so the survivors will so badly want to retaliate, you will just get richer, fatter. Meanwhile, Anderson's people take the fall. And once they uncover the Swiss account in his name — how there only seem to be deposits in it from a Middle Eastern routing number — the same routing number as your former account in the Middle East — everyone will think that al-Qaida or Hezbollah was funding them. People will want to retaliate on the Middle East and you will be able to help."

"Spent some time on the phone with the bank, did you?"

"Yeah."

"Pulled the old 'I work for the FBI' shtick and they shit their pants I bet."

"Something like that."

"You are so predictable and that's why it was so easy. All the same, I applaud your detective work. What, did you get the clue off the latest sound byte?"

"Yeah."

"Then the bank."

"And after the bank it was just a matter of making the connections."

"That's one thing I have to give you, Will. I tip my hat — you were always a great detective… but you were never very good at seeing what was right out in front of you."

"Neither were you."

Strughold laughed, winked. "Right. I really am impressed with your skills, though, Will. Really. You were a little too late to do anything about it, but knowing you, getting to the truth was its own reward."

"Jesus Christ, Martin, you're capitalizing on the death of millions — here and overseas — for the sake of some money. That's... inhuman."

"It's not just some money, Will. It's a lot of fucking money. And a legacy to account for." Keeping a beat, Strughold made himself a drink and downed it. "When I became the CEO this place was a joke. *A fucking joke.*" In front of Besson, behind the desk again. "In just ten years I brokered big deals in the Middle East and now with the United States military. Add on the nuke disaster's aftermath — the contract will definitely go through, I get my money and the government gets its revenge.

"And can you see the history books? Can you *see* them, Will? The chapter about this ordeal — a picture of me in the corner that reads: 'Martin Frederick Strughold: hero and patriot who provided the weapons for which we used to fight and defeat the enemy.' Now that sounds mighty fine, don't you think, Will? Sounds pretty damn good."

"So money and a line in a textbook. That was your price?" Besson asked, disgusted. "Giving a good name to war profiteering?"

"I'll remind you of the comment you made. You know, 'taking advantage of the deaths of millions,' or some shit like that. I'll ask you to take that, and take the money incentive away, take a look in the mirror one day and tell me if you see anything familiar."

Smaller, his head down, Besson whispered, "You son of a bitch." Looking back up, "Fuck you."

A smirk. Slowly, savoring, "No, Will. Fuck. You. How many have already died — and how many millions more will die — by your means? For your ends?" Normal again, "Tell me that, Will."

"I am nothing like you."

"If you really believe that you're still as blind as we agreed you were."

"Do you know what a wilderness of mirrors is, Martin? It's a term used in the intelligence community for an operation that has become so convoluted that it becomes impossible to discern truth from untruth."

"And you think we're in that wilderness now?"

"I think you are that wilderness." He paused. "I used to look up to you. You know the way I grew up. I looked to you for a father, you son of a bitch."

"Ohhhh. Is that what this is about? Betrayal by the surrogate father? Though I'm not surprised you looked to me that way. I wouldn't say it was such a bad choice. We are very similar. You coulda been my own."

"I used to fight people like you. I hated people like you." Distant — a realization. Besson said, "When you stare long into the abyss—"

"The abyss stares back at you," Strughold finished.

Besson put his head down again. Strughold looked at him and was reminded of a child. The sound of a click brought his gaze back to level, staring down the end of a 9mm. "You're going to kill me now?"

"I have to, son."

"Don't you think people'll find it strange — blood, bullet holes and a corpse in your office?"

"It's a holiday weekend. I'll have Lavalle and the others come and make sure it's cleaned. No one will ever know. We'll make a new detonator, set the bomb off and no one will even consider the idea of a murder in my office when there are millions dead outside of it. Hell, there won't even be an office left after all of it's through."

"Every detail, right?"

"Always."

"You know it's funny. You said that I miss what's not in front of me. And you know what, maybe we aren't that different because you're the same way."

"That a fact? What did I miss, then?"

"The Bureau teaches you to keep a round chambered."

Besson veered left, out of Strughold's shot. He wrapped his right arm around Strughold's extended gun hand, slamming it down as he threw his left hand up into Strughold's elbow. He yelped — a left hook silenced him, making him fall back into his chair.

Besson, SIG back in hand, pointed it at Strughold, who was holding his right arm, covering bare bone, his nose trickling blood, his fingers broken.

"Even if you stop all this, Will," Strughold forced between groans, his eyes concentrated, screaming, "we'll still have one thing between us."

"What's that?"

"In the end, if there is a Heaven, neither of us will ever see it."

Solemn, receptive. "I know."

That damned smirk. "*Quod sum eries*, William."

"Not anymore."

Strughold's curtain call — a single muzzle flash, and a thick curl of blue smoke danced from the gaping hole in his head. Besson watched as it veered and twisted upwind, flittering, thinning and eventually dispersing, exiting the world. Besson stood over the corpse for a moment, looking into Strughold's lifeless eyes and felt no specific feeling towards it.

He recovered his clip, chambered a bullet and re-holstered it on his way out the door.

41

Despite Jansen's repudiation of the idea, Hamlin ordered that she be accompanied by Jim Dormer as well as a tactical team going to all the places that Besson might show up.

The two partners and the tactical team drove over in an unmarked black van, destined for Besson's Whitestone. They drove over in silence, all of their minds stuck on the mission objective. Hamlin had been good enough to leave Jansen's connection to their suspect out of his report to the other agencies as well as the FBI.

"Helluva way to spend Christmas Eve isn't it?" Dormer said. Nobody replied. "I thought you were on vacation," he said to Jansen.

"Hamlin called me in." It occurred to her that Dormer might have remembered her mentioning her boyfriend was a former FBI agent — a fact that made it to Besson's profile that had been sent out to DHS, and the CIA. This would explain Jansen's sudden reappearance, as well as her sudden change in behavior — tired, drained and uncertain. Dormer's suspicions seemed to have a quality of prior knowledge, but he himself seemed also to be rather distracted. It was hard for Jansen to determine if he had made the necessary connections or if it was a mere observation. Dormer himself was also someplace else, deep in thought.

No one said a word for the rest of the ride over. Jansen felt a beam of red sunlight bounce on her eye. She looked to see two bullet holes that hadn't been covered by stucco or spackle. She lowered her head to avoid it, and realized that in a half hour there would be no sunlight. There would be the dull harshness of a winter's night. She hoped that the darkness would last the duration of the night.

Besson's apartment was cold, as if someone hadn't been there in quite some time. Jansen knew he wouldn't be there.

The Forensic team found no traces of radiation once they arrived on scene. The apartment was tossed, sparing no closet or crevice. The search was desperate.

The landlord came up to inquire about the commotion, and was met with a search warrant.

Jansen stayed out of the way, as if lost in a foreign place. She didn't care if anybody called her on it, or to her connection to this place or its former inhabitant. For the first time in years, she wasn't sure of what her next move would be.

Pieces of old conversations rankled: *"I miss the rush I used to get, cracking the case, catching the guy. I love the satisfaction I got from knowing that person won't hurt any more people with what he was doing. Cases are like a big puzzle, and I had to put the pieces together and figure out how things fit. I learned that more times than not, if you pull the right string, the case comes loose and reveals itself.*

"It's the famous buildings — symbols of what makes us stand out. The only one left, really, is the Empire State Building. Everyone knows that building, and it's a sign of forward progress."

"My God," she whispered to no one.

She placed the picture down as it had been originally, and silently slipped out of the apartment. She hailed a cab.

"Empire State Building."

Jansen walked up to the secretary at the front desk in the lobby of the Empire State Building and flashed her badge. She then showed her a picture of Besson.

"Have you seen this man at all today?"

The young woman — grad student probably — looked at the picture for several seconds. "Yes I did. The FBI agent. He said he was sent over to check with security — it being the holidays and all."

Jansen's stomach sank. "Where did he go?"

"He took the service elevator down to the boiler room. He said he had to talk to the maintenance worker. I told him he was off today, but he said he was going to check down there anyway."

"How long ago was this?"

"Five minutes ago."

Jansen nodded and thanked her, and ran to the service elevator. Once inside she drew her service weapon and tried to keep her hands from shaking.

The slamming of the boiler's shell onto the ground was loud enough to drown out the sound of the service elevator touching down on the floor, and its doors opening.

Besson came face to face with the fully functional bomb. It hummed and seemed to pulsate as Besson opened a small keypad in the center. This keypad had been installed by Dr. Moira Grey in case of this kind of situation.

Besson typed the necessary password to override the PDA's system, then typed in the original code. The countdown started up again from where it left off, then made up for the elapsed time. He dialed the next code — the code overriding the countdown signal. Two buttons lit up, one green and one red. They flashed and then steadied. He had to press only one.

He hesitated. His finger was moistened by sweat. He was teary eyed, but rationalized that this was the life he chose —the path he chose. The path this city chose.

To his left side, he heard the faintest of sounds. His coat flew open, and he turned, moving for his SIG at the same time. He had just taken the SIG from its holster, but Jansen already had her Glock trained on him.

"I'm not as fast as I used to be," he said dryly.

"Don't do this, Will."

"I have to. You know that."

"Why?"

"Because it's the only way to make things change; the only way to make a difference."

"No it's not. We took the same oath..."

"We both know that people like us can never make a real difference." He pointed at the bomb. "But people will undoubtedly *learn* from this."

Jansen's grip was slipping. Besson was slowly motioning back towards the bomb. She stiffened her grip and Besson froze again.

"It doesn't have to be this way," she said.

"Yes it does."

Both of their eyes gleamed.

"What about us, Will?" she choked. "We could've been happy."

"That's why I brought you to the Poconos. I wanted to save you from this. You're one of good people — one of the things that makes this world beautiful. I didn't want you get caught up in... *this*."

"A lot of good people will die if you go through with this. Innocent people. Like Sarah, that girl you told me about."

"They'd be the sacrifice; dying for something bigger than themselves. We've both seen this: good people sometimes have to die in order to compel change. Sarah was different."

"No she wasn't and you'll be destroying a lot of the beauty in this world if you detonate the bomb."

"...all for a greater cause," he replied weakly.

"You're doing this for all the right reasons, Will. I mean that honestly. But to do this, you've killed innocent people. You've aided terrorists — men and woman that help to destroy the beauty that you advocate."

"I had no choice. Sometimes you have to get dirty — play by their rules — to get things done."

"Then why not me?"

"What?"

"Why not sacrifice me the way you're *sacrificing* everyone else?"

"Because I love you. Because I've lost everyone I've ever loved and I couldn't let it happen again."

"But it is happening, Will... it's happening again. How many people are going to have to lose the ones they love because of what you're doing tonight?"

Besson considered this for a moment — the comment scathed him.

"What about your parents, Will? What would they think of you now?"

Besson's face was grim. He put his head down.

"This isn't you, Will. You're a good person. You don't want things to end this way."

Lifting his head up again, he stared at Jansen, his face dark.

"You're not going to shoot me. I know you won't shoot me," he said. He turned his back to her and walked back to the bomb.

"You told me your biggest fear was to see kids grow up just like you did. But, after today, how many are going to grow up like you? And how many will grow up to *become* you?"

Besson had stopped, staring deeply into the red and green buttons on the keypad. Behind him he heard the Glock reverberate as it hit the floor and Jansen beginning to sob.

Green. Red.

Green. Red.

Green. Red.

Finally, red.

Then, there was stillness.

"I-I couldn't do it," he whispered, turning back to her.

She clasped him tightly and they held each other, both weeping gently.

"I'm sorry… I'm sorry. You were right."

"You can't be here," she said, when they separated.

"I know."

"You'd better go."

"What about you?"

"I have to stay here, Will."

"Come with me." He was pleading.

"Not like this. I'm going to make sure they won't come after you. I can redeploy the team at your apartment someplace else — let you get your things together."

"Let me handle—"

"Please, Will, just go."

He nodded and started away from her. They were shoulder to shoulder, back to back, when she grabbed his hand. They froze there for several seconds, and they turned to each other slowly and awkwardly; sincerely kissing one last time. Time itself seemed to stop in that moment. They were the only two people left on earth… it was familiar. They both knew this would be their last encounter, that in order for things to be set right, their love would have to remain unrequited.

42

Besson left. Jansen stayed behind and gathered herself. She held her cell phone in her shaking hands and dialed once they stopped. She cleared her throat.

Hamlin answered.

"It's Andrea."

"Jesus Christ, where the hell are you? We're on active protocol and you're—"

"It's over."

"Excuse me?"

"The bomb has been deactivated."

"And Besson?"

"You better get down here. Empire State Building. And have Jim and his team follow you."

Hamlin arrived first, and confronted her. His anger turned to relief, once he saw the dormant bomb.

"What happened?"

"I know him. I came here and we talked. *He* disarmed the bomb."

Hamlin didn't hide his shock.

"And where is he now?"

"On the lam."

"You let him go?!"

She began to tear again and said, "I couldn't shoot him."

Hamlin nodded and hugged her. "I understand."

"It's not over yet," she said.

"What do you mean?"

"I need to speak with the President."

Hamlin and Jansen sat in Jansen's office for over an hour. The sky was dark; the city was bright and alive. There was an appreciation of the pulsating city among the law enforcement agents involved in this evening's events.

Hamlin had his hand reached across the desk, holding hers. She took little comfort. It was too early for that.

Dormer entered the office awkwardly.

"When we got back to Besson's apartment, the place was cleaned out. Pictures, clothes, everything. His bank account was cleared out too. But we did find this." Dormer placed an audio tape on the desk. "It wasn't there at first. We think Besson left it."

"Has anyone listened to it yet?" Hamlin asked.

"Not that I know of."

"Thank you, Jim."

He lingered.

"Is there something else?"

"President Ellison and the SecDef are on a live video feed in the conference room. They want to speak with the both of you."

Jansen and Hamlin filed into the conference room and sat down.

"I'm told that the bomb threat has been negated," Ellison said.

"That is correct, sir," Hamlin said.

"I and the President would like to thank you, Agent Jansen, for your excellent work especially considering the circumstances."

"I was told that both of you were made aware of my connection to Mr. Besson," she said.

"Yes, I was briefed on your..." Ellison searched for the word. He decided finally on "relationship." He made it sound wrong. "What do you have, agent?"

"A recorded confession from W... from Besson."

"We already know he's guilty."

"Sir, it's for something else."

"For what?"

"Immunity."

"You must be joking," Ellison said. "William Besson is a traitor and a—"

"Sir, with all due respect, I do believe you both should hear the contents of that recording," Hamlin interrupted.

"Have you listened to the recording, Agent Hamlin?" Kersh asked.

"Yes I have, sir, and I think it's important that it be played here now."

"May I?" Jansen asked.

Ellison nodded hesitantly.

Jansen pressed PLAY.

"My name is Will Besson. I will have it known as of now that I am under no duress and I am not under any kind of coercion. I am speaking of my own free will. After parting ways with the FBI following the drug bust in El Paso two years ago, I began working for Halifax, working directly under Martin Strughold. We devised a plan to detonate a nuke in Manhattan. As it turned out Strughold's plans were, in truth, much darker than mine and I had no choice but to act. You'll find more information on his work computer.

"Using my accumulated knowledge of intelligence that I had been able to take from the FBI database I helped this organization steal a hydrogen bomb from the military. It was in that assault that each member of the convoy was killed. I, myself killed one of the soldiers."

Jansen put her head down for a moment.

"I also was the sniper that assassinated Frank Crowley last month. In my time working with Strughold, I worked with the following people: Dr. Moira Grey, Marcus Gardner, Josh Anderson, Martha Dench, Christopher Gavin, Peter Lavalle and Ted Lomax. The leader of Sons of Liberty also — despite our assumption — was not Josh Anderson. It was Martin Frederick Strughold — who I myself shot earlier tonight. Josh Anderson's attack on the Manhattan Bridge was meant to fail because of his attempts to take control of Sons of Liberty. Strughold needed him to die in such a way that would help us — make the bridge look like the primary objective — and have the other members of his militia think he died heroically.

"I was set on detonating the bomb with the idea that it would give the survivors a better appreciation for life. I was doing it out of love for my — this — country..."

"We have seen the enemy and he is us," Ellison said softly.

"...*I was afraid of a continuing downward spiral, but I understand now that what I was doing was wrong; although you may not believe me, it's true. After September 11th, I decided to change with the harrowing times in which we were suddenly living. I went too far. All I wanted was to avoid more needless tragedies in the future. My intent was to turn people off to these horrors — to make them revolt against this kind of violence, to know the misery of this kind of life.*

"*My methods were faulty and you won't have to worry about seeing or hearing from me again.*

"*I would understand if you want to take me in and try me for my crimes — but we all know the implications of not only making this official, but also of public knowledge. For all intents and purposes I will simply disappear. In exchange for this information I'm hoping you'll take this as a sign of good will. Thank you.*"

The recording ended and the room stood silent.

"I want a full investigation launched on Peter Lavalle, Martin Strughold and Halifax. See if Besson was telling the truth," Ellison said to Hamlin.

"Yes, sir."

"Agent Jansen, do you know where Besson would go on the lam?"

Corsica, Luxembourg, Marseilles, Gibraltar, Brussels, Marbella, Provence. "No idea, sir."

"What about Will?" Jansen asked, no longer caring about the informality. He was more than just a name to her.

"I want him found and prosecuted. He's a traitor and a murderer," Ellison reiterated.

"Sir, it's not that simple," Jansen said. "Just as he stated in the recording, the implications of that would be severe."

"Are you speaking as his proxy?" Kersh asked.

"Yes, sir, I am. And if I may point out: Will doesn't want to fight anymore. He won't be coming back. If this whole thing gets out, it'll make the Robert Hanssen situation look like a joke. The FBI will go down the drain and no one will trust the government. Finding and prosecuting him will only hurt us." Jansen was well versed in the concepts of Realpolitik. "Not too many people of weight know about all this. We can still keep this quiet. Suppose Will Besson was working undercover, on behalf of the White House which had launched an investigation on Martin Strughold."

Ellison absorbed what she had said. He considered having Besson silenced; his sense of morality told him otherwise. Besson was an American; regardless of what he had done. He did not want his office to accept cold-blooded murder as a deterrent or solution.

"Do you believe that Besson will stay true to his word?" Ellison asked.

"I do, sir."

"And what do you think, Al?"

"I think she brings up several valid points; but at the same time I think Besson could still be a risk if he stays free. Either way we'd be taking a huge risk." Kersh sighed. "However, Agent Jansen knows him better than any of us. If she says he'll stay quiet, I think it best to leave him be."

"Alright then. Besson will have his immunity. I'll send the papers through momentarily."

"Mr. President, there's also the matter of Peter Lavalle," Hamlin said. "The news has already gone public with the fact that there was a bomb threat in the city. If Lavalle knows that Besson wasn't killed he may step up his attack. He may try to find Besson — make him talk. If he turns Besson in our victory will be marred by the level of Besson's treason."

"Then we'll spin *another* story," Kersh said. "That there was an American involved but he had been killed trying to detonate the bomb."

"Good," Ellison replied. "That's good. Bill, I want you to head this up." He would have Hamlin gain as much information on Lavalle as possible, and have HRT deployed when he was finished.

"Now there's the matter of this office," Kersh said. "With Agent Graham unable to remain in charge, the burden falls upon you, Agent Jansen. Despite what's happened, you've proven your abilities and your devotion to your country. Would you like the job?"

Jansen shook her head after several seconds. "I would like a transfer. Anyplace outside of New York." Her voice was low. She padded the edge of the table with her palms. "Preferably a desk."

Hamlin deliberated. "The London office has a SAC position opening in a month."

Jansen knew the motive — the further out of the way the better. "Thank you, sir."

"Who's going to fill Graham's place now?" Kersh asked. "Who's the next in line?"

"That'd be Jim Dormer."

"Is he competent?"

"I believe so, sir. Very hard worker," Hamlin vouched.

"Then he can fill the role on a provisional basis and see how he performs."

"I'll tell him, sir."

"Are you sure this is what you want, Agent Jansen?" Ellison asked. "There is a glory to this kind of victory — it was all your work that saved New York."

"A glory that costs everything and means nothing."

43

The excitement at the office finally died down around eight, but because of the new responsibilities he had to prepare for — the paperwork, a quick overview of the duties he would have to perform, as he was briefed by Bill Hamlin and Alan Kersh — Jim Dormer didn't return home until ten. He opened the door with a sense of relief.

Eileen heard him close the door behind him and met him at the entrance to the kitchen.

"Presents are under the tree."

"Good work," he said with a smile. He grabbed her around the waist and put his hand in hers. "Come on, baby, let's dance." He moved around with her, swaying around the kitchen as she struggled to break free.

"…Off me, you fuck."

Dormer clasped tighter.

With her free hand she slapped him across the face — "Ackkhh!" — and he finally let go.

"What the fuck is wrong with you?" she asked.

"Not a damn thing," he replied chuckling.

She handed him the papers that were on the kitchen table. "I want a divorce."

"You got it, baby."

"You know, I'm surprised you showed up tonight. You haven't been home since you caught me fucking Conner."

"That's right, but I've had a great day."

"The news said there was a terrorist attack averted. Did you have something to do with it?" she asked in a pseudo-interested voice.

"I was part of the investigation, which succeeded."

"I'm glad it faired better than your marriage," she said, with a sudden burst of sarcasm.

"That was cold, baby. But, to answer your question—"

"I didn't ask one."

"—I'm home because I want to see my daughters."

"Saying goodbye?"

"Don't count on it." He moved closer to her. "It seems that my boss is… *incapacitated.* They offered me his position on a provisional basis and I'll keep the position if they're pleased with my work over the next six months which also means—"

"You'll be working even later—"

"Early in the morning to the early evening. I'm going to hire an assistant so I can see my girls."

"Still late hours."

"I won't be in the field."

"That isn't—"

"Shut your fucking mouth, I'm not finished yet!" Then, resuming a normal tone, "And if you even think about taking my daughters, I'll just let the judge know that their mother hasn't worked since Squeaky tried to pop Ford—"

"Don't exaggerate—"

"—and that their father is the Assistant Director of the FBI's New York office. Who do you think the judge'll side with then, Sugar?"

"You fucking asshole."

"Blame bin Laden. We're hometown heroes now." Dormer chuckled again as he headed for the door. "Merry Christmas, ya hateful bitch."

44

Andrea Jansen had been slipping in and out of a daze the entire afternoon. She had originally thought it was a side effect of the chloroform,, but now she knew better. In the span of just a few hours she had learned there was a nuclear weapon in Manhattan, was almost killed by it, was transferred from her job and learned her boyfriend was involved in the crisis that she had prevented. Despite all that, it was only the matter of Will that lingered in her mind. Her thoughts traveled to him, and she would be lost in that daze once again. She wanted to hate him but she couldn't, regardless of what had happened. She knew she wouldn't be able to sleep tonight.

She stepped off the elevator in her apartment complex and walked down the hallway to her apartment. On the doorknob hung a leather jacket. She knew whose it was, but was still taken aback. It smelled like him.

She took it inside with her and threw it on the couch, and noticed it made a strange sound once it landed. Going into the kitchen, she unearthed a bottle of Canadian Club, poured some into a tumbler, and began what was to be an all night affair.

Sitting on the couch, she glanced at the picture of her mother.

At least I know Will loved me, Jansen thought wryly. She realized then that in the last few months whenever she thought about her father, the memories no longer affected her. Good riddance.

Jansen drank while watching the news and was relieved not to see Besson's face plastered all over it.

She looked over to the leather jacket and decided to investigate what had made the odd sound. There was something in one of the pockets.

A box from Saks Fifth Avenue and a letter.

She opened the letter first. It was hand-written, and had been done after he deactivated the bomb.

Andrea,

Although you may never believe me, and you may never understand what I did — I did it with the best intentions; but then again, as the saying goes, the worst things in history began with the purest intentions. Or something like that.

The wit wasn't totally lost on him, even now.

In hindsight I wish I could take it all back in exchange for what we could've had. You represented the life I always wanted, and in doing this I think I robbed the both of us of it. I hope that you accept my apology. I guess I'm really good at screwing things up between the two of us, and once again I guess we could say 'the circumstances were the circumstances.' Life really does come full circle, doesn't it?

This time, she actually smirked.

I see now that my actions were wrong. The importance of and need for peace is a lesson that cannot be taught by force, but through life experiences and the uninterrupted passage of time. The creating, maintaining and prospering of peace is a charge we must all take a part in, and it is a charge that should not be one man's burden. The methods I had planned on creating peace would have destroyed a great deal of the beauty that I was promoting, and I have you to thank for showing this to me, Andrea.

I know what I did to you was wrong; I shouldn't have gotten you caught up in my world, but you did exactly as people like you do: you made things better. You represent the people in the world that I wanted to save.

You made me into a better person.

I wish I could say 'when next we meet' but we both know that's impossible now; yet again, a fault of mine.

Besson knew that if his involvement with the attempted terrorist attack were made public, the damage to the FBI would be exponential. Besson also knew that although the bomb did not go off, the details that were leaked to the press would make it to the news and then into the public's awareness.

In the days and weeks that come to pass, I hope you'll come to forgive me and I hope that you know that you very well could be the best thing that has ever happened to me, and I'll never be able to pay you back for that, and while I know my credibility cannot be very good right now, I would like to ask one last thing of you: don't be like me. Stop running.

I will never forget you or the times that we spent together. They were the best I've had. I'll love you in my dreams.

With love and gratitude always,
—Will

The tears that fell from her eyes were no longer tears of frustration and anger, but of loss. Her resentment for Besson began to dissolve and when she felt the strength to, she opened the box. It was a locket in the shape of a heart. She opened it revealing two pictures. On one side was a picture of him, the second of her.

The picture had been taken early on in their rekindled romance. She had admitted to him that she had never been to the boardwalk at Coney Island. He took her there, along with a camera. They had lunch at Nathan's and sat on the benches overlooking the beach. Somebody passed by and offered to take their picture, noticing the camera. They obliged, despite Besson's initial reluctance. She had forgotten about that day, and the picture. They were smiling rather sheepishly, and she smiled now, reliving the memory. She felt something on the back of the locket, closed it and turned it over. Etched into the gold was a short statement that read: MARKED IN DAYS BETTER SPENT.

Not unlike the night she spent talking to her mother before leaving for college, Jansen again learned the divine faculty of forgiveness.

Thinking about her absentee father again, the memories no longer hurt — they didn't matter. That hurt was gone, and soon enough this hurt would fade too. That was the true gift Besson gave her. He taught her to accept that past sufferings could be alleviated.

She didn't move from her couch, and continued to watch her television long into the night. To her surprise she began to nod off, and she wrapped herself in Will's leather jacket. A final, conciliatory truth surfaced in her final moments before sleep: that they would be tied together forever, their hearts shared, a legacy that would outlive them both.

45

An unburdened Will Besson waited in Grand Central Station for his train, set to depart at midnight.

He carried with him a duffel bag packed with his bank savings and the advance money Martin Strughold had paid him; as well as some personal keepsakes. The station was still sparsely crowded due to the late hour on a holiday. Besson fit in perfectly with the crowd, not an unkind eye among them. Andrea Jansen had in fact saved him from the wrath of the federal government. A smile meant only for him drew upon his features momentarily.

As he prepared to leave the city he buried what remained of the distasteful acts that had been visited upon him through means that held him accountable and those that were not. His parents. Ludlow Kealty. Manolo Cervantes. The nameless soldier. Carl McDowell. Martin Frederick Strughold. He resigned them to the past, and decided to leave them there.

He could not, nor would he, let go of Andrea.

Looking at the celestial sphere design of the ceiling, its inaccuracies purposely made to give spectators a view of the sky that only God has, Besson wondered how God had felt watching and having to accept the bloody actions of His creation. Besson wondered how he would have felt watching from that same point of view as his city burned, screamed and went dark. A pang of shame kept him from wondering too long followed by a sense of relief. His role in this was over. And that was Andrea's final gift to him.

It was up to others now. It was up to the rest of us to consider what happens in the great change that was going to come when news of the bomb threat comes to light. We'd promise change. And we would. And it wouldn't last. Besson knew this from experience. He measured the ability of the human spirit and contemplated its ability to change, truly, when faced with tragedy. The answer, of course, was, it couldn't.

He turned back as he reached the stairway leading to the lower concourse and track as if to give a final nod to his past before walking away from it. He again looked at the ceiling—the unchanging precession of equinoxes, the single dark patch that was never remodeled a reminder of the past. The four faced opal clock told him it was midnight.

The train in which he traveled was almost completely empty, just a handful of people who were sleeping. Most passengers were trying to make it to their families by Christmas morning. Some would make it, while others would not. For Besson, the only one in the train car still awake, it was the first step in a longer journey.

He looked out the window, at the trees quickly moving past. As snow began to fall he stared intently, and listened closely to the symphony playing over the speakers, compliments of the conductor. The sullen and morose instruments were emphasized with a dull, dreary sadness, creating a sense of dread in the pit of his chest. Slowly, an underlying, lighter piece began to play under the heavier blanket. Besson could feel both of the pieces working in harmony; he was absorbed by the symphony's beauty, and allowed himself to be warmed by it.

As his mind would eventually linger too far, and he would eventually sleep through the night, Besson would be met in his dreams at the beach he had almost forgotten. The beach of pale sand, caressing sunlight and the stifling beauty of a rippling cerulean ocean that lay in front of him, which paid tribute as the most sublime, untouched region on earth. Besson's thoughts drifted one last time back to the life he was leaving, and all he had lost: his parents, his friends, his home and Andrea Jansen—the love of his life. He did know, however — as she did — that the life they had shared together was one that couldn't have lasted after this day, that what they had was something that was swept under the tide's current as it raced out to sea, into distant memories that can be found in the Remembrance of Days Past. Theirs was a world they could not maintain.

From here, he would voyage out to the world outside of what he knew. He would travel to one of those places where the pace of life was slower, where a man could wake up and walk around town and not see a skyscraper, where the news didn't dictate the criterion of the day's events, where politics were discussed only in passing conversation, and in only speculative terms. There would be satisfying work, and streets of cobblestone where children played, unsurpassable. There would be cordial weather, glasses of fine wine, sumptuous meals, and beaches where the sands were white and the ocean laid out before him was cerulean.

He would meet a well-cultured and intelligent native woman. They would go out into unremitting dewy evenings and dance to orchestras on verandas, consume wine and make amorous love. When the time came they would adopt children. In truth, there was no way to keep them from the reality of the world they lived in, but he had no intention of lying to them. He would do as he imagined his parents would've done for him: teach them the conduct of good people, and guide them the best he could through life, love them and make sure that they knew that at home, they were welcome, and that they were safe.

He would be remiss if not to doubt a place like that was truly out there, but he had time. He could spend his life getting there. Besson would find a place for himself in the world and when he reached his final impasse he could reminisce on his completed journey, the people he had gained, loved, lost, what he was leaving behind, and feel a sense of completion. When his time came, if there was something beyond, in the clear light of Hereafter, he would see her— Andrea — ageless, untouched by time, her memory easily recalled.

"I shouldn't have done those things." he'd say.

"That was a long time ago,"

She would nestle her face in his outstretched hand, closing the curtain one last time, and usher him forth. He would look back only once and then press forward, good-bye to all that.

Printed in the United States
209049BV00001B/251/P

9 781934 925522